Six winners. Six fantasies.
Six skeletons come out of the closet...

Plain Jane Kurtz is going to use her winnings to
discover her inner vixen. But what's it
really going to cost her?

New girl in town Nicole Reavis is
on a journey to find herself. But what *else*
will she discover along the way?

Risk taker Eve Best is on the verge
of having everything she's ever wanted.
But can she take it?

Young, cocky Zach Haas loves his
instant popularity, especially with the women.
But can he trust it?

Solid, dependable Cole Crawford is ready to
shake things up. But how "shook up"
is he prepared to handle?

Wild child Liza Skinner has always
just wanted to belong. But how far is she
willing to go to get it?

Million Dollar Secrets—do you feel lucky?

Dear Reader,

With reality TV the rage these days, it seems everyone wants their fifteen minutes of fame. Imagine what it would be like to be in the spotlight five days a week with your own TV show...and get paid to talk about sex and relationships! What's not to like?

For my heroine, Eve Best, this is the world she knows and loves. The only problem is, she's all talk and getting no action—until a sexy network scout shows up and everything turns upside down. While writing this book I considered TV stars and the difficulty they have in maintaining a private life—not to mention balancing ambition with love. Find out how Eve does it in *The Naked Truth*.

For more, be sure to visit my Web site, www.shannonhollis.com.

Warmly,

Shannon

SHANNON HOLLIS
The Naked Truth

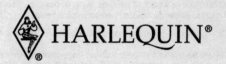

HARLEQUIN®

TORONTO • NEW YORK • LONDON
AMSTERDAM • PARIS • SYDNEY • HAMBURG
STOCKHOLM • ATHENS • TOKYO • MILAN • MADRID
PRAGUE • WARSAW • BUDAPEST • AUCKLAND

ISBN-13: 978-0-373-79354-9
ISBN-10:   0-373-79354-5

THE NAKED TRUTH

Books by Shannon Hollis

HARLEQUIN BLAZE

144—HIS HOT NUMBER
170—ON THE LOOSE
203—SEX & SENSIBILITY
254—FULL CIRCLE
331—NO RULES

For Meline and Russ, with gratitude

_1_

"So WHAT'S IT going to be? Sexy secrets? The best lies lovers tell? Or should we find someone with a confession to make?"

Eve Best looked into the faces of the production team for _Just Between Us,_ the afternoon cable show she hosted on CATL-TV. The show that had just been profiled in _Vanity Fair._ The show that was rocketing up the ratings and making the dreams of everyone in this room come true.

Every Monday at five, they got together in this conference room to hammer out the roster for the following week, with the exception of Fridays, when she invited a panel to take questions in a town-hall meeting format, or she simply did it herself. But for four twenty-two-minute segments, Monday through Thursday at three o'clock, they had to come up with the best in sexy, cutting-edge topics and guests. The funny thing was, no matter how many shows they did, they never seemed to run out of material.

They were, after all, talking about human behavior, in all its wonderful forms and mutations.

Lainie Kaye, the junior of their two segment producers, waved a sheaf of clippings. "If we go for a guest, I got a commitment from Dawn Penney. She's the actress, remember, who turned a part in that awful horror movie about the beach resort into a career character. Now she writes that column for the *Register,* 'Perfect Dates.' *Sex and the City,* Atlanta style."

Eve made some notes in her planner. "Get her. See if she can do Thursday."

Cole Crawford, their executive producer, looked up from the binder that went everywhere with him. Eve had asked him once if he slept with it under his pillow, and had been immediately sorry. Since his wife had up and left him, the topic of sleeping with anything or anyone was a sore one. Cole had made his kids and his career his whole life—to the benefit of the show and the detriment of any hope of a love life for the poor guy.

"Wednesday would be better," he said. "Hump day and all. Get people past the middle of the week, right?"

Eve shook her head. Technically he had the last word on programming, but this was her show. And the more popular it got, the more clout she had and the more it was likely she'd get the programming she thought audiences would respond to best.

Not a bad place to be, considering Cole was one of the few who remembered she'd started out as junior weathergirl back in the day.

"Thursday," she repeated firmly. "When Thursday hits, people start thinking about plans for the weekend. It's the perfect time to hear about the perfect date." She sat back, satisfied, as Cole nodded and gave in. Lainie left the room at a jog, as if Dawn Penney would give away the space they needed on her calendar if she didn't get to the phone this second.

"Okay, three down, one to go," Eve said. "What are the possibilities for Wednesday?"

Nicole Reavis, their primary segment producer, had her own sheaf of clippings. "I had an idea the other night about male-female communication," she said. "What if we get someone like Dr. Deborah Tannen, the linguistics expert? She could talk about the differences in communication styles, and how what we say isn't always what the other person understands."

"I'm liking this," Eve said. Cole leaned forward. A good sign. "Go on."

"We could focus on subtext," Nicole said. "You know, what I'm saying isn't really what I'm talking about, and how that gets us into trouble in relationships."

"Trying to read the other party," Cole said. "How to find out if they mean what they say. Maybe even negotiation tactics and how that works in relationships."

He would know. But Eve kept that to herself.

"Let's do it. Nicole, get one of the coordinators to find the guest—someone local, if you can—and you and I will work on the script. And how about we carry over the theme to the Friday town-hall meeting? I bet everyone in the audience has a miscommunication story. We'll pull three or four out to give advice from a male and female point of view."

"Consider it done." Nicole scribbled frantically in her notebook.

Just then, Zach Haas, the youngest crew member but the most experienced cameraman, poked his head into the room. "Sorry to interrupt, guys. Cole, those camera tests are ready whenever you need them."

"Thanks, Zach," Cole replied, and the twentysomething kid disappeared.

"So are we finished?" Eve looked around the table. "Yes? Good job, everyone. See y'all tomorrow."

As the noise level rose with people pushing in chairs and collecting their stacks, Eve's assistant pushed through the rush for the door. "Eve—"

"Hey, Dylan."

Dylan Moore was six feet tall and thin as a licorice whip. With the ink still fresh on his communications degree and dirt from the family farm in south Georgia scrubbed off his toes, he was determined to have a career in television and didn't care how humbly he started. Eve was sure to lose him to Cole one of these days. She'd resigned herself to that. But in the meantime, he was the one who kept her functioning from minute to minute. He'd probably learned project management by default from all those years of being the eldest of all the sibs in the picture on his desk.

"He's here," Dylan said in a low voice, tugging on her elbow to draw her away from the door and, presumably, the foyer where guests at the station waited.

"Who?"

But she already knew. Had been dreading his arrival from the moment Cole had told her about him the previous week.

"Him. The exec from CWB." Dylan glanced at the door, but the room had emptied. At the confirmation of her fears, Eve felt a trickle of dread settle in her stomach. "Mitchell Hayes. The guy who wants to eat you up and have the rest of us on a plate for dessert."

UNDER THE CUSTOM-TAILORED suit, Mitchell Hayes tried to roll the tension out of his shoulders. Every muscle seemed locked in place, which made it tough to look relaxed and confident.

In this business, appearances were everything—it was bad enough in New York, but that rule had probably been invented right here in Atlanta. This afternoon, it was vital that he look confident without being arrogant. Not to mention friendly and trustworthy and sincere without looking like a suck-up.

"If we can get *Just Between Us,* we'll have the female demographic locked up," Nelson Berg, his boss at CWB, had said two days ago. "You get this Eve Best to sign with the network and you'll be golden."

"And if it doesn't work out?"

Nelson had given him a long look and tented his fingers over his stomach in a way that meant bad news was coming. "We asked you to sign Jah-Redd Jones and NBC got him. We needed—not just wanted, mind, needed—Alastair McCall's *Animal Mind-Hunter.* And what happened there?"

"OLN had a mole in the station," Mitch had protested. "McCall was signed up before I even got on the plane."

"Well, they don't have a mole at CATL-TV," Nelson had snapped, "but it's only a matter of time. Eve Best is ripe for the picking, and this money she and her friends have won in the lottery is a ratings gold mine.

You get down there, romance the socks off her and her staff and get them signed up."

"Or?" Mitch had said before his brain had a chance to catch up with his mouth.

"Or I'm going to have to replace you." Nelson's face had been kind, but the words were brutal. "Not much point in keeping a scout who can't bring home the bacon, is there?"

No, there wasn't.

On trips such as these Mitch often wondered why he did this. Why he put up with Nelson's crap. Nobody on the guy's staff had a life—they were so busy bringing home the bacon they didn't have homes to go to. Apartments, yes. Places to keep their stuff, sure. But homes? Nope.

Something moved behind the soundproof glass wall that backed the receptionist's desk, and the card-secured door clicked open. An African-American guy who could have made a career in college basketball stepped out.

"Mr. Hayes, I'm Dylan Moore, Eve Best's personal assistant." Mitch shook his hand. "Right this way."

Mitch followed him into the rabbit warren of corridors, taping booths and offices that made up TV stations all over the country. This one boasted three studios—one for news, one for network linkups and a huge one for the exclusive use of *Just Between Us*.

As he passed behind the backdrop that somehow managed to convey a sense of home along with big-city glitz (who was their set designer?) he had to smile. Because of course the studio was all about appearances, too. Behind the set, where the camera never went, the walls were naked board and batten, with schedules and notes stapled all over them. Tie wraps secured wrist-sized bundles of electrical wiring and cables to the studs, along with Ethernet and T1 lines.

It looked so like the studios at CWB that he felt right at home. Or at least, as much as a guy could feel at home when he was living in a pressure cooker.

At the top of a set of stairs, he passed a conference room, where, from the debris, it looked as if a production meeting had just ended. Moore paused at the door of an office next to it, and Mitch resisted the urge to stretch his neck muscles one more time and straighten his tie.

He nodded at Moore and walked into Eve Best's office with a smile and an outstretched hand.

One of their affiliates in Atlanta had sent him a box full of DVDs of the last three months of the show. But even watching forty hours of Eve Best hadn't prepared him for the reality.

She pushed her chair back and came around the desk to meet him—and his entire body went on alert. It was as if his pheromones met hers in the space between them, and exploded in a chemical reaction. The small screen simply didn't do justice to the curves and the healthy glow of her skin. Her baby-doll top was cut just low enough to show a tempting swell of cleavage but not enough to be in bad taste. He'd expected that triangular, girl-next-door smile that knocked viewers off their chairs, but it didn't happen. Instead, he got the full effect of those wide, long-lashed green eyes.

And they weren't particularly glad to see him.

"Eve, this is Mitchell Hayes from CWB," Moore said from the door. "Mr. Hayes, Eve Best."

"Thank you, Dylan." Her voice, which was husky and playful when she spoke to her guests, was merely husky now. Subdued or not, it stroked some pleasure point deep inside Mitch's chest. In fact, the whole package seemed to be custom-made to stroke every pleasure point he had—and when had been the last time he'd experienced that?

What had Nelson said? He was here to romance the socks off this woman and get her to say yes.

To the contract.

He needed to focus on his goal, and soon, or he'd be in the deepest trouble of his career.

"Please sit down, Mr. Hayes."

Belatedly, he realized he needed to say something to take control of this interview and stop drinking her in like a teenage boy staring at the head cheerleader.

"Thanks for seeing me, Ms. Best," he said. "I know your schedule is probably packed."

"You're right there. The only place I could fit you in was at the end of the day, and even at that I need to keep it short. I appreciate you've come a long way to have this conversation, but I'm going to a benefit this evening. I'm afraid I'll need to leave in about half an hour."

What an amazing voice. What charisma. No wonder the viewers were flocking to *Just Between Us*. He could watch this woman all day. "That will be plenty of time." Once again, he tried to convince his body to relax. But his body was far more interested in hers than it was in getting her commitment to the network.

And then she smiled. It wasn't an I'm-glad-to-see-you smile, or a come-on-over smile. It was an I'm-going-to-break-this-to-you-in-the-nicest-possible-way smile and his concentration went straight to hell anyway.

"It doesn't take long to say no, does it?" she agreed sweetly.

Get it together. Your job depends on the next half hour. "I'm hoping I can convince you otherwise, Ms. Best. Communications and Wireless Broadcasting is prepared to make you a very generous offer in hopes that you'll sign on with us, a national network, and bring your talents to our wider viewership."

"Please call me Eve. Everyone does."

He smiled. For a fraction of a second, her gaze dropped to his mouth, and a tiny spurt of gratification deep inside him celebrated it. "And I'm Mitch."

"How long have you been with CWB, Mitch?"

His rational brain recognized that she was dodging a reply. His irrational brain was happy to make small talk as long as she wanted to, if he could keep listening to that voice.

"Coming up on five years. I started out in production, but then realized I was better at the business side. I was always tripping over cables and walking in front of the wrong cameras."

There was that smile again. A little warmer, this time. "Do you like being a scout?"

"Yes." *I used to. Now I'm not so sure.* "I like bringing people who deserve it to the attention of people who will love them. Like you, for instance." Neatly, he brought the conversation back around to the reason he was there. "If you'll bring your show to our network, we're prepared to offer you six million for the first year, eight for the second and ten for the third if you'll agree to sign with us."

A slow blink was her only reaction. For a woman whose openness and frankness were her trademark, she evidently knew how to be as cagey as a poker player. "That's very generous."

"You won't find a better deal, even with the big guns like NBC or SBN. Have they approached you?"

"If they had, I'd hardly say so, would I?"

Of course not. CWB had its spies, and they'd have been careful to brief him beforehand. But that didn't mean the bigger networks wouldn't be hot on his heels once they heard CWB was courting Eve. Television fed on itself, after all.

"Maybe not, but you know how it is. Everyone knows everyone, and word gets around."

"Well, the word around here is no." With a glance at the clock, she rose. Mitch got to his feet as she again came around the desk and held out a hand. "Thank you for taking the time to come and make the offer, Mitch. It's very flattering, but the answer is still no."

He took her hand, and two things registered. First, that her fingers were slender and warm in his. And second, that she was taller than he'd thought. He stood six foot three in his socks, and with the strappy heels she wore, the top of her head came almost to his eye level.

Then a third thing registered. She smelled delicious.

A combination of vanilla and spice and the clean scent of warm skin. Involuntarily, he drew in a breath, and she looked into his eyes.

"Mitch?"

His brain went blank. He murmured some vague words of thanks for her time and then beat feet out of there, finding himself in the driver's seat of his rental car before he knew quite how he'd gotten there.

And a good thing, too.

Because if he'd stayed one second more, he'd have pushed Eve Best up against the wall of her office and breathed that scent from the side of her neck. Then he'd have kissed her senseless.

He could only imagine what *that* would have done to his chances for getting her to say yes to him.

He shook his head as if to clear it. To CWB. Not him. To CWB and their offer.

Yeah. That's what he meant.

2

"WAS THAT HIM?"

Jane Kurtz leaned in Eve's office doorway and, when she saw that Eve was alone, slipped inside and shut the door.

"Yes, that was him." Eve gave up on trying to organize her desk for the following day and leaned back in her chair as Jane sat in the one reserved for guests.

The one he'd just vacated.

"His name is Mitchell Hayes, and he's with CWB."

"Oh, I like them. I watch *Dirty Secrets of Daylily Drive* every week."

"Jane, we are not *Daylily Drive*. And we are not signing with them. I told him so and he vanished like a puff of smoke. But he'll be back."

"How do you know?"

"By the pricking of my thumbs." And the humming in her ears. Not to mention the tingle of possibility deep in her belly, where it had no business being at all.

"Just how accurate are your thumbs?" Jane straightened a pile of research clippings on the corner of Eve's desk. When Was the Last Time You Got Some? the headline on top wanted to know.

Eve resisted the urge to throw the latest issue of *People* on top of it. She didn't want to think about that. She spent sixteen hours a day thinking about relationships, and men and women, and who was getting what and why, and whether they'd come on the show to talk about it. It covered up the uncomfortable fact—which she devoutly hoped no one else noticed—that she, Atlanta's relationship expert, did not have one.

She bet Mitchell Hayes had one. Two. More. In fact, he probably had every eligible model and aspiring actress in New York lining up at his door. Well, she wished them luck. Mitchell Hayes wasn't getting her show—or anything else, for that matter.

"Eve?"

She blinked and focused on Jane. "What?"

"I said, how accurate are your thumbs? Is this Hayes guy going to take you at your word, or are we going to have to get Jenna to take out another restraining order?"

Jenna Hamilton was the station's attorney, and after the recent announcement about their $38-million lottery win, she'd already had to take out two restraining orders because things had gotten out of hand with an unruly fan and an angry truck driver with a nonwinning number. Once the news had gotten out about the protectiveness of the legal team, the number of nasty letters in the daily mail had dropped. Thank goodness.

Even yet, two months after the win and the press conference and all the hoopla, Eve still had a hard time believing that there could be seven or eight million bucks in her future. With that kind of money, she could buy some property outside of town. Travel. Do more than dabble in philanthropy. The only real problem they had was the lawsuit against the five of them, filed by her and Jane's former best friend, Liza Skinner, demanding her fair share of the loot since they'd played her number. The whole subject caused Eve so much pain that she did her best not to think about it.

Again, she focused on answering Jane. What was the matter with her? Her mind was jumping around like a bean on a hot stove. "He's on a mission. The network has tasked him to poach me away from here, and he's going to do his best to do it. He won't take no for an answer at first. I can tell."

"He looked like a player, all right."

For some reason, this rubbed Eve the wrong way. "I wouldn't say he was a player. Not in the sense you mean. But he's got a stubborn chin and there's no dummy behind those eyes. He's serious about this. The network's talking big money."

Jane waved away the thought. "Who needs it? We're going to be set up for life. And what are you doing looking at his chin?" As soon as Eve saw Jane's gaze narrow on her, she realized her mistake.

She shrugged with a pretty good imitation of nonchalance. "You know me. Always sizing people up. Reading them. Trying to figure them out."

Not looking at lips and wondering what they'd feel like in a deep, hot kiss. Not sneaking peeks at long-fingered hands and wondering how they'd feel on skin. Nuh-uh. Nope.

For once Jane took her at her word and got up. She must be a better actress than she thought. "I'm glad I don't have to deal with him, then. You can always make yourself unavailable and sic Jenna on him."

"I already did." Eve got up, too, and collected her briefcase. "Make myself unavailable, I mean. I have the Atlanta Reads benefit tonight, remember? I just hope nobody remembers I wore my green dress to the Women of Power fund-raiser, as well."

"Put some peacock feathers on it like Nicole Kidman," Jane suggested over her shoulder, already on her way back to her own office. "Or heck, zip downtown and get yourself a new one. By the time you get the bill, we'll have settled the suit and you can buy a different dress for every night of the year."

Eve laughed and shook her head as she pushed open the employee exit door and headed for her car. That would be the day.

Lottery winner or not, she couldn't see herself shaking the careful habits of someone who had grown up with not much more than the basic necessities of life. Isabel Calvert, her maternal grandmother, who had taken in a traumatized eleven-year-old after the death of her parents in a car accident, had still been working as a Realtor. Though they lived in Coral Gables in a tiny stucco house with an orange tree, money was tight and Eve had learned to be practical along with how to turn out a decent meal and do her own laundry.

Not that those were skills to scoff at. They'd stood her in good stead through university and during her move from Florida back to the city her father's family had called home for generations. And during the early years, when getting the job as associate senior meteorologist—

aka junior weathergirl—had seemed like the apex of her life, she'd discovered she not only had a knack for throwing dinner parties on the cheap, but for digging out and retaining all kinds of information about people.

A great skill to have in this business. But it didn't help her with a dress for tonight.

With careful investments, she'd managed to save enough for a down payment on a little house in the Vinings district. Nana would be proud. It wasn't very big—in fact, it had once been a carriage house on a much larger estate—but it certainly had a good address, and in Atlanta, that was half the battle. With the worst of the rush hour traffic clearing, she made it home in record time. Which, of course, left her lots of time to shower, do her hair and contemplate her closet.

She had all kinds of things to wear on the set, some courtesy of Jane's wardrobe budget and some of her own. She had jeans and camis to wear on weekends. But a couple of black dresses and the green one could only go so far. Now that she was starting to make the society pages, maybe she should take Jane's advice and run up her credit card on a couple of evening dresses. If what Cole predicted came true, she was going to be spending even more time in the spotlight. Thank goodness for the lottery—because she'd bet her winnings the station wouldn't be picking up the tab for her updated wardrobe.

The green one would have to do. It fit like a glove— though she watched her weight like a predatory bird, her hourglass figure would pack on a pound in a heartbeat. And everyone knew the camera packed on twenty in less than that.

A final spritz of hair mist and her grandmother's diamond chandelier earrings, and she was good to go.

The benefit for Atlanta Reads was being held at the Ashmere mansion. The property had recently been made the headquarters of the Ashmere Trust with the hopes that it could become a moneymaking venture while it retained its Old South beauty. As far as Eve could tell, they'd succeeded in a big way. She stepped out of the cab and the soft, warm evening air caressed her bare shoulders. She draped the green chiffon wrap over one arm and breathed in the scent of ferns and mulch and eucalyptus from the gardens.

Straightening her shoulders, she mounted the fan of steps and swam into the crowd, turning to greet society belles and financiers alike with the grace of a dancer and the confidence of three years in the spotlight.

"Eve. Glad you could make it."

Eve turned to see Dan Phillips, owner of both the station and the production company that produced *Just Between Us,* at her elbow. "Hey, Dan. I had to come. Who wouldn't want to support helping people learn to read?"

"People in television," he said, so deadpan she couldn't tell if he was joking or not. Which was par for the course. "My wife forced me into my tux and out the door at the point of a nail file."

"Maya's a smart cookie," Eve told him. "You won't regret it. I hear Ambience is catering."

"Really?" He brightened. "Then I guess I should start schmoozing. I do like to hear people talking about you behind your back, anyway."

Eve held up a hand. "Just don't tell me if it's negative."

"It won't be. Everyone in Atlanta loves you." He paused. "And a few people up north, too, from what I hear."

Eve didn't pretend to misunderstand. "I'm going to assume you spoke with Mitchell Hayes."

"I did."

"And?" She prodded when he took a sip of his martini and didn't go into detail.

"And nothing. It's not my decision, it's yours. Though I made it clear that the show belongs to Driver Productions and if he managed to get you, it would be only at the end of your contract. The show stays here, though what it would do without its host is another headache."

"You won't have to worry about that. I told him no."

Phillips looked her full in the face for the first time. "Did you, now?"

"Of course. We're doing just fine right where we are. We have great facilities, happy advertisers, and we're building the viewership in leaps and bounds. Why should I upset the applecart and risk everything on a young network that's still trying to prove itself?"

"Because it might be the right thing for your career?"

Now it was Eve's turn to stare at him. "Tell me I didn't hear you say that."

He shrugged. "I've known for at least a year that the big boys would come knocking. It's what every regional host wants, Eve—a shot at the national level. CWB is handing you that on a platter. I wouldn't blame you for jumping at it—though it might be best to wait for more of the networks to offer. Make the station an affiliate as part of the deal."

Maybe he wouldn't blame her, but how could she? They'd built a terrific team here, from Jane in makeup to Cole in production. If she agreed to go with any network, what would happen to all of them? They were practically family. The new organization would probably bring in all its own people and move her somewhere else. She'd get national exposure but she'd never see her friends again. She'd already experienced being the one who was left behind. No way would she do that to someone else if she could help it.

"You won't have to worry about it, Dan," she said. "I told Mr. Hayes no, and I meant it."

"I'm sure you did." His gaze caught on something over her shoulder. "But I think he means to make you change your mind."

Something in his tone warned her, and she turned just in time to see Mitchell Hayes pause on the stairway. He had one hand casually on the polished banister, the other in his pocket, hitching up the jacket of his tux in a way that turned formality on its ear and made it sexy.

What in the world…?

He scanned the crowd lazily, and two seconds too late, she understood what he was doing.

He was looking for someone—and she had no doubt whatsoever who it was.

THE MOST DIFFICULT THING any of these people had to read was probably their bank statement.

Mitch knew he was being a reverse snob. His own

paycheck was pretty generous, considering he hardly ever had time to spend any of it, but his annual salary was probably what some of these folks paid in income tax.

His gaze moved from one part of the vast marble foyer to the next, noting a thumb-sized emerald here, a designer suit there, a pair of skyscraper stilettos somewhere else. One thing was for sure—he needed to move to a room where the acoustics were better, or his head was going to split from the sound of high-pitched laughter and conversation shattering on the stone all around him.

He ducked into the nearest room, which turned out to be the location of the buffet, and exhaled in relief. There was no hurry. He didn't even know if Eve Best was here yet, and he had nothing else to do except catch a movie on HBO back at the hotel. It had taken less than thirty seconds online at the local newspaper's Web site to find the society listings, and from there to narrow down the field to the three that he'd define as a "benefit." The other two were for sports and health care, so he'd gambled that a woman who made her living by communication would have a connection with people who communicated with words on a page—and those who were learning to.

He'd give this an hour. If he was wrong, at least he had the sports gig to look forward to.

The same connection at the affiliate station who had sent him the DVDs of Eve's show had also done some calling around and come up with a spare ticket for this one. He owed her big-time, especially if he succeeded in convincing Eve to come to the network. In fact, a blue box from Tiffany would probably be in order.

Which showed how important it was that CWB get this show. Nelson would probably sign the requisition without even blinking. Or reading it.

He heard someone laugh behind a huge urn filled with stargazer lilies, and he inhaled sharply. After forty hours of recordings, he knew that sound. A strange feeling swooped through his gut, and he stepped cautiously to one side, peering around the flowers.

And there she was, heading for the buffet with an elderly woman, a polished older man and a woman with a neck like a swan. Or a ballet dancer. His gaze dropped to the woman's feet, which were turned out. Yep.

He'd dated a dancer from the New York City Ballet for six weeks the previous year. He'd discovered about five weeks in that Analiese was much more beautiful onstage as a swan or a princess than she was as a girlfriend, so they'd parted amicably and he'd bought season tickets to the company's performances. It was the music he liked best, anyway.

Eve and her companions filled plates that weren't much more than wafers of china, and stood by the windows visiting and eating hors d'oeuvres. Mitch took a flute of champagne from a passing waiter and then stopped him.

"Who's that, do you know?" He nodded toward the window. "That couple talking with Eve Best."

The waiter glanced at them. "Don't know who the old lady is. But that's Roy and Anne Best with Eve there. Must be related. He was a developer before he retired. Put in that new retail complex in Decatur. Word is he's looking to buy a share in the Thrashers." His gaze swung to Mitch. "Too bad they didn't make the playoffs this year. You follow hockey?"

"Sure do." Hockey, soccer, snowboarding. Anything but football or baseball, a preference that would probably get him hung in one or two southern states. "Thanks."

"Enjoy your evening, sir."

Roy Best moved slightly, giving Eve an unobstructed view of the window, which reflected the brightly lit room.

Mitch realized that he was standing in that reflection at about the same time she did. So much for lurking behind the flower arrangements while he waited for a moment to speak to her alone. She turned, and the light slid along the silk folds of her strapless gown, which crisscrossed across her breasts and hips, throwing every curve into perfect relief before it cascaded in folds to the floor.

She looked like a goddess.

A really angry goddess.

She said something to her companions and stalked across the floor to where he stood next to the lilies, and he braced himself for thunder and lightning.

"I saw you when you came in, Mr. Hayes. How did you get in here?"

"I'm fine, thank you, Eve. You look beautiful."

Her step hitched in surprise, and then she recovered. "Thank you. If you're following me, the answer is still no."

He managed to arrange his face in an expression of mild surprise. "I wasn't, actually. I have a ticket, bought and paid for and arranged in advance."

Okay, so two-thirds of that was true.

She narrowed her eyes at him and looked so completely touchable that he had to put his champagne down on the nearest table and stuff his hands in his pockets. What he really wanted to do was reach out and run them down her bare arms.

"I don't believe you."

He reached into his jacket. "I have it right here if you want to look at it."

"No, of course not. Fine. Enjoy yourself." She turned to walk away.

"And I'd heard such great things about Southern hospitality," he said with regret to the nearest lily.

That stopped her. "What's that supposed to mean?"

"Only that I'd expected you to be a little more gracious in a social situation. Given your reputation for making people feel at ease and all. It certainly comes off on the screen."

"Are you implying that I'm not making you feel at ease?"

She made him feel hot and slightly out of control and hornier than he'd felt in at least a year. "You could say so." A pause. "Not that it matters. We only met today. Please." He indicated the couple by the window, now chatting with a couple of guys in suits. "I don't mean to keep you from your friends."

"That's my grandmother—my father's mother—and my aunt and uncle." The words came out slowly, as if she were reluctant tó tell him anything personal, but now felt as though she had to in order to be polite.

"Are they here from Florida?" Again the narrowed eyes. "I did my research, Eve. That's where you grew up, right?"

"Yes. And no, they're not. All my dad's family is here in Atlanta."

His face relaxed into the first sincere smile of the evening. "It must be nice to have family so close. All mine are in New Mexico. I'm lucky to see them once every couple of years."

"Planes fly both ways."

"They do," he allowed, "but after the November sweeps, things go crazy. I can never get out of New York during the holidays."

She nodded slowly. "I know. Before she died, I only saw Nana—she's the one who raised me—in the summer during our hiatus, and Florida in July is, well…"

"I know." He took a breath as he caught a tune floating over the sounds of conversation. "Not to change the subject, but would you like to dance?"

"Dance?"

"Yes. An ancient rite performed in praise of the gods." He surprised her into a smile, and his concentration fell into pieces. "My God, you're beautiful," he blurted.

Then he gave himself a mental slap and waited for her to walk away.

3

MITCH NEVER LOST CONTROL. He was always calm, cool and unbiased…which, now that he came to think of it, hadn't been standing him in good stead lately. Was that why his last two bids for shows had fallen through? Because he hadn't shown enough passion for the chase? For them?

Was that why his longest relationship in the last couple of years had topped out at six weeks?

Was that why he kept striking out with Eve Best?

But instead of rolling her eyes at his ineptitude, or sidestepping away as though he might be a stalker, Eve smiled again.

"That's the first honest thing you've said all day," she said, then held up a finger. "No, the second thing. The first thing was about your family in New Mexico. I'd love to dance. Thank you."

Relieved and slightly dazed at this reversal of his expectations, he offered her his arm. She took it and they followed the sound of Duke Ellington into a massive glassed-in conservatory that had been converted into a ballroom. At one end, a big band played, perspiration trickling down the faces of the guys blowing trumpet and trombone. Fairy lights glittered in swaths along the wrought-iron ribs of the ceiling, and palm trees stood at intervals along the walls, with the windows opened to the night air. It felt like something out of the twenties, when mad young things danced the Charleston and the world held every possibility.

Maybe his world held possibility, too, Mitch thought as he whirled Eve into a spin and then took her in his arms. And he didn't mean for business, either. Tonight he was an ordinary man dancing with a desirable woman, and he would leave business out of it and enjoy every second.

"So how long are you going to make me wait?" she asked.

The green silk of her dress moved gently under the hand he had flattened on the small of her back. Besides the heat of her body, he felt the movement of toned, controlled muscles and the beginnings of the curves of her hips.

"Wait?" He'd oblige her in the nearest closet, if she wanted.

"For CWB's counteroffer. Didn't you come here to talk business?"

Oh. He'd forgotten all about CWB.

"No. I came to contribute to Atlanta Reads. And to ask you to dance."

"One out of two isn't bad," she murmured. He spun her into another turn and whirled her back. "Not that I believe either one."

"Literacy's a good cause," he said. "My pet charity is Music on the Street."

"Mmm, that's three honest things. Tell me about it."

"It's a grassroots organization that teaches inner-city kids an instrument. They play in a band that gives concerts on basketball courts, in gyms, wherever they can get space. We fund the instruments and the teachers, because the schools can't."

She leaned back to look into his eyes, and his thinking ran aground on that clear green gaze.

"What's your instrument?"

He nodded toward the band. "Trumpet. Or it used to be. I've been racking up so many frequent flyer miles I'm way out of practice."

"Security would probably confiscate your horn as a dangerous weapon, anyway," she said with a twinkle. The music segued into a slower number and instead of thanking him and leading the way off the dance floor, she fit her body closer against his. He slid his arm farther around her waist and tucked the hand he held against his shoulder.

Whatever witty and self-deprecating comment he'd been about to make fizzled away into soundlessness. All he could think about was how good she felt in his arms—how warm and silky her skin, how intoxicating her scent. The weight of her breasts against his chest and the brush of her thighs as they moved together across the dance floor were making him crazy.

Making his body temperature rise.

And that wasn't all.

"Mr. Hayes, I'm shocked," she whispered, her lips close to his ear.

He had two choices. He could make a break for the

door and hope he could bribe his way onto the next flight to New York, or he could brazen it out and hope the sense of humor she displayed on TV was real and not put on for the camera.

"I am, too," he whispered back. "Usually I'm much better behaved than this. But then, I've never danced with you before. Now I know I have limits."

She giggled, tried to choke it back, then seemed to give up. She threw back her head in an honest-to-God laugh. Both arms crept up around his neck.

"I meant I was shocked you weren't going to counteroffer." Her voice wobbled with laughter.

Oh, no. Could he just go into cardiac arrest right here and now? Maybe if he went out on a stretcher she'd look at him with pity instead of...what was this?

Her face was alight with humor, not malice or derision. And in her eyes he saw appreciation and a lowering of her guard.

"Mitchell Hayes, you win the prize."

"And what would that be?" he asked, trying to keep his head up in a sea of embarrassed misery.

"You've told me five honest things in the space of half an hour. That's more than I've been able to squeeze out of half the guests we have on the show—and a lot more than I usually get out of the men I've dated."

He huffed a breath of laughter and tried not to think about the way her arms were looped around his neck, bringing that delectable body even more flush against him. "So what's the prize?"

"We're going to start over. You don't scout for a major television network, you never came to my office.

I've just met you and learned that you're from New Mexico, you love your family, and you play the trumpet and want kids to enjoy music the way you do."

"You left out the fifth thing." What was it his dad used to say? In for a penny, in for a pound.

She shrugged, and flashed that enchanting triangular smile. "Your body's very honest, too," she said. "I like that in a man."

JENNA HAMILTON read the brief one more time in the cab: *Skinner v. Best, Kurtz, Crawford, Reavis, Haas.* The rolling in her stomach was due less to reading while in motion than to the simple fact that this was the biggest, most public case she'd ever had to handle.

And she wasn't sure she could do it.

No, no. Scratch that. She'd learn as she went, and get the best advice she could find. She'd already read every scrap of case law in the online library—and she'd branch out to libraries in other states if that's what it took to win this case.

As the station's corporate lawyer, and a junior lawyer at Andersen Nadeau who had her eye on a partnership some day, this was her chance to shine. Eve and the others expected her to pull it off, and she wouldn't disappoint them if she could possibly help it.

The cab pulled up outside the offices of Kregel, Fitch and Devine, which had once been a brick warehouse but was now part of the trendy Decatur district. She paid the driver and took comfort in the knowledge that she knew the details of Liza Skinner's suit inside out and backwards. Not only that, the file rested in her Kate

Spade tote. If there was ever a secret weapon designed to give a woman confidence, it was that.

When the receptionist caught sight of it a moment later, she straightened and announced her right away. The butterflies in Jenna's stomach settled down. Maybe it was a sign of things to come. She took a firmer grip on the handles and followed the young woman into a spacious office that had enough of the warehouse's bricks and pipes left showing to give it an edgy, industrial look while screeching "major interior designer" at every turn.

A tall man crossed the room, his hand outstretched.

Nice suit, was her first thought.

Nice hands, was her second, as Kevin Wade shook hers.

"Thanks for coming, Ms. Hamilton," he said, his voice a smooth bass that tickled something deep inside her. "My client and I appreciate your willingness to be flexible."

His café-au-lait skin was just a shade lighter than hers, and his brown eyes held a male appreciation that made her body sit up and take notice. No, that wasn't it. Her spine was straight to give the impression of control, not because it would throw her breasts into prominence. Nuh-uh.

"We might be at this for a while," she replied, "so please call me Jenna."

"And I'm Kevin to my friends."

She didn't bother to point out that *friends* was the last thing they were—or were likely to become. Too bad. But with this much money at stake, it was far more

likely they'd wind up on either side of a courtroom, each doing their best to grind the other into defeat.

Instead of seating himself in the power position behind the desk, he waved her over to an area by the window that contained a couple of couches facing each other across a low, square coffee table. Some case law and several manila folders already lay on it, as though he'd been doing the same thing she had in the cab.

As they went through the points of Liza Skinner's lawsuit, she realized that he was darned good at his job, and that this was more of a challenge than she'd anticipated. If only she could focus on the numbered paragraphs of the filings instead of the way his long-fingered hands lay on the papers, or the way she'd get a whiff of his delicious cologne every time he got up to fetch a highlighter or a box of paper clips. This was not going to win Eve and the team what they wanted.

She reined in her errant thoughts with a stern hand. "Kevin, I'm afraid that's not going to be acceptable to my clients," she said after he reiterated Liza Skinner's position on one particularly irritating paragraph in the brief. "The fact is, the lottery winners are not willing to cut her in on a share of the money—nor should they have to. It's regrettable that they and Ms. Skinner didn't think to set down the terms of their agreement in writing before they bought the tickets. But without any kind of contract, it's impossible to hold my clients to what she's demanding."

"They were friends," he reminded her. "Would you make your friends sign something before you gave them tickets, say, for a birthday gift?"

"This wasn't a gift," she said. "They all played the same number each week and they all went in on it together—except for Ms. Skinner. She was out of town, out of state—out of my clients' lives permanently, for all they knew. Any reasonable jury would see that her claim is groundless."

"It can't be groundless if there was a verbal agreement," he pointed out. "She may not have told them she was leaving town, but she never told them she was leaving the group."

"Regardless of whether she told them or not, I think her departure managed to state it pretty effectively."

"But metaphors don't stand up in court."

He smiled at her, and Jenna lost her focus. That smile had probably gotten what he wanted out of every judge in town. Well, it wasn't going to work on her.

"The members had a verbal agreement, and Ms. Skinner contributed to the pot." He pointed to the relevant paragraph in the complaint.

"They won *after* her monetary contributions ran out," she reminded him, pointing to the paragraph that countered his in the brief she'd filed that week. "My clients may have played what she's calling 'her' number out of a sense of friendship, but in practical terms, she herself was not a party to the win. She can't *own* a number."

"The fact remains that they threw money in the pot in her name, playing the number she played consistently—as you pointed out—over a period of time. She was a virtual member of the group, whether she was there physically or not, and deserves a share of the winnings." Kevin Wade's tone was firm. "The case of *Barnes v. Hillman* sets a precedent. I'm sure you've read it."

Of course she had. She'd read every single piece of case law connected with state lottery winners in the database—texts that had kept her up past midnight for more nights than she could count. "*Barnes v. Hillman* isn't relevant to our case," she retorted. "In that case, the widow filed on behalf of her deceased husband, who was part of a group. Even though Georgia isn't a community property state, for the judge it was open and shut."

He leaned back and extended an arm along the top of the couch, for all the world as if he were giving her an invitation to join him.

Which was crazy. *Focus, girl.*

"*Bradley v. Tillman, Morton and Ramirez,* on the other hand, sets a precedent for our case." She riffled papers until she found the one she wanted. "It was proved conclusively that unless all the group members agree in writing that they're going to play their numbers together, the money can't be distributed to anyone else."

"Mr. Bradley, unfortunately, was a resident of another state that doesn't allow lotteries," Kevin said. "There wasn't much the judge could do about that one."

Okay, so she just hadn't found a precedent that applied point for point to their case, but she would. Just give her time.

"So where does that leave us?" Jenna resisted the urge to tap her papers together and be the first to concede a standoff.

"I don't know about you, but it leaves me starving.

I didn't get a chance to have lunch. Do you feel like going somewhere to eat?"

A second too late, she realized she was "catching flies." She snapped her mouth shut. "I don't think that's appropriate, considering we're on opposing sides of a case, Mr. Wade."

"You called me Kevin before."

"I think it's time to reestablish some distance," she said steadily, though her heart was bumping erratically in her chest. She dated a few guys on a casual basis, but no one seriously. She was just as likely to go dancing with a bunch of her girlfriends on her rare nights out. Certainly none of the guys she hung out with, most of whom had been her brother's college buddies, had this sense of masculine power and casual authority that was drawing her into its seductive net, one breath at a time.

Kevin glanced at his watch. "Come on. It's after seven. What difference does it make if we talk over the case here and go hungry, or talk it over at Cioppino and enjoy great Italian? It's just a couple of blocks away, and it's a nice night for a walk."

Cioppino. She'd heard a couple of the partners talking about it and it sounded heavenly. And when would she have time to spend an entire evening there? Probably never.

"Fine," she agreed. "But let's set down some ground rules. Namely, we split the bill."

"Done."

As she tapped her stack of briefs together, Jenna added another ground rule to the list: no lusting after him. Because no matter what happened with the case, breaking that rule would get her into the most trouble— guaranteed.

EVE COULDN'T REMEMBER ever having had such a good time at a fund-raiser. A lot of events such as this involved chatting up people she didn't know, trying artfully to get them to pull out their checkbooks or posing for the media or attempting to jazz up the obligatory speeches after dinner. But this one…it was like being the prom queen. Not that she'd ever been the prom queen, mind you. She'd been too focused on her SATs and getting into university and from there out into the real world.

But tonight, everyone conspired to make her feel desirable and sought-after and at least five pounds lighter than she actually was. Or maybe it just seemed that way because Mitchell Hayes managed to snag her for one dance out of every three. Then two dances…and then she found herself dancing with him exclusively. But it didn't really matter, because it was close to midnight, the media had gone, and everyone with fat checkbooks had trickled out the door. That left the under-thirty-five crowd to take another run at the buffet tables and convince the band to play something less vintage.

She didn't care what they played, as long as it had a beat and she could slip in and out of Mitch's arms as he whirled her out and back. His hands never strayed where they shouldn't, but each time he touched her, slipped an arm around her waist or took her hand it felt like a caress. Like a man touching his lover with that focused attention that told her he had plans for her later.

Which, of course, Mitch didn't. At least, she didn't think he did. And even if it were true, really it was impossible. She wouldn't sleep with him under any provocation, simply because of who he was and why he was in Atlanta. But he was a fabulous dancer and after a couple of flutes of champagne she felt loose and happy and ready.

For what, she wasn't sure.

Oh, to dance—that was it.

Without being obvious about it, he'd managed to dance her over to the French doors and out onto the terrace.

"We can't hear the music as well out here," she objected.

"The band is going to be packing up soon." Still holding her hand, he led her over to a shady corner where ivy cascaded down the exterior wall. It smelled like green cinnamon, and the hem of her dress rustled on the flagstones of the terrace, echoing the way the breeze rustled in the trees. "I need some breathing space. You wore me out."

She leaned on the stone balustrade. "I doubt that. You strike me as a man of endurance. You probably run marathons in your spare time."

"If I had spare time, I'd do something less masochistic." His voice warmed with a smile as he leaned beside her. "Back home, if I wasn't doing something related to music, I'd ride my dirt bike in the pine forest. I never made it up to the top of the sandstone mesa behind our house, but I spent a lot of summers trying."

As he spoke, he moved behind her. She felt his warmth down her back as his arms slipped around her and held her, loosely, giving her the choice to pull away.

Or not. She settled herself against his chest, her head leaning on his shoulder as they looked out over the darkened gardens. Tomorrow she'd remember that he was CWB's scout and probably didn't have her best interests in mind. On Monday, when he reappeared in her studio, she'd send him on his way with another firm no.

But tonight belonged to her and Mitch, their careers and worries stripped away, leaving only this elemental desire and the sense of anticipation and possibility that thickened the air.

She felt his warm breath on the side of her neck a moment before he tasted the bare skin where neck met shoulder. His tongue was hot and he took his time, as though kissing her there were all he had to do for the rest of eternity. Eve sucked in a breath and felt a jolt of pleasure arrow through her. Her nipples tightened, and her breasts seemed to swell in the satin prison of her strapless bodice.

"Do you like that?" he whispered against her skin.

"What if someone sees us?" she breathed.

"It's dark over here." He kissed her again, moving an inch up the side of her neck. "No one can see a thing. And you didn't answer me."

Now he nibbled her earlobe, running the tip of his tongue just behind the post of her earrings.

"Yes." He pressed against her from behind, and even through her skirts she felt the hard demand of his erection. "You're being honest again," she whispered.

"I can't help it. I've been holding you all night and doing math equations in my head so I don't embarrass myself on the dance floor. Again."

"And now?" She knew she was being deliberately provocative, but she couldn't stop. Okay, she wasn't going to sleep with him, but there was nothing wrong with flirting. Nothing wrong with appreciating the attention of a very attractive man.

"Circumference equals two pi R," he murmured. "No, that's no good. It just makes me think of—" He stopped.

"What?"

"I don't want to spoil the moment by having you slap me."

"I promise I won't. Tell me."

"Circumference makes me think of round things. Which doesn't help my situation."

"What things?" Her voice had gone low and throaty. Who knew that talking about geometry could be such a turn-on?

She could feel his breathing change rhythm now. "Oh, things hidden from view in green satin. Very round, very beautiful, very distracting things, for instance. Among others that don't even have geometric definitions. They need to be explored. Measured. Mapped for posterity."

Amazed at her own daring, Eve took both his hands in hers and slid them up her bodice until they cupped her breasts. "Tell me about how you measure," she said.

He made a choked sound and his hips surged against her backside, pinning his erection against her softness. Under her fingers, his hands tented over her breasts, gently squeezing and shaping…and inadvertently pulling her bodice down until his sharply indrawn breath beside her ear told her that, from his vantage point, he'd just caught a glimpse of her nipples.

And she wanted his hands on them, wanted his mouth, wanted him to suck and lick and drive her wild with desire. Wanted him to throw her skirts up and drive himself into her right here on the terrace, where she'd brace herself against the balustrade and take every hard inch of him into the vast, soft, dripping ache inside her.

Oh, God, what was she thinking? Was she crazy?

As if he'd heard her thoughts, he hooked his thumbs inside the whalebones of her bodice and pulled it up to a respectable level. He dropped his hands to her waist and stepped back. "Eve, I'm sorry. I didn't mean for things to go that far."

She turned, and realized that she was partially in the light from a window overhead, while he was in the darkness next to the ivy. All she could hear was his labored breathing.

"I know," she breathed. She arched her spine, so that the bodice slid down a few precarious millimeters and her cleavage became even more pronounced in the golden light. "You make me want things I shouldn't."

You're teasing him, a voice in the back of her mind warned. Don't do it if you don't mean to go through with it. Stop while you still can.

"Likewise," he said hoarsely. "More than anything I've ever wanted in my life. But not here, where anyone can walk out and see us. My car's here. Come back to my hotel with me."

Balancing on the scalding edge of desire, Eve teetered and fell.

4

HE COULDN'T GET her into the Lexus fast enough. What were they, a pair of horny teenagers desperate for privacy? Mitch fumbled with the rented car's keys and managed to get them into the ignition on the second try. Then he made the mistake of glancing to the right—and he was done for.

Eve leaned toward him, her eyes hot with desire and her lips parted. One arm wound around his neck as he crushed her mouth under his in a kiss that told both of them how much he wanted to be somewhere horizontal right now. She made a noise deep in her throat, like a purr, as her tongue met his and slid along it in sensual invitation, stroking its length and making his imagination go wild.

What couldn't a woman with a tongue like that do to a man's body? He felt himself stiffen even more at the thought.

She broke the kiss to nuzzle the soft skin below his ear. "My nipples are so hard," she breathed. "I want you to touch them."

He didn't ask why the about-face. He didn't want to know. All he knew was that they were both under some kind of spell—both crazy to have one another despite the fact that it was unethical and probably fatal to his mission.

"I will," he promised fervently. "As soon as we get out of here." The Ritz-Carlton, where he was staying, wasn't far.

"I can't wait that long. Now."

"No, we—"

She moved her shoulders in a slow-motion shimmy, and the green bodice slipped down about an inch as she leaned toward him. His protest died on his lips as her breasts swelled out of their confinement. He couldn't have shifted his gaze if he'd tried. With another breath, the silk slipped some more and twin shadows appeared above the rims of the cups.

"Touch me," she whispered.

He pulled her toward him and captured her mouth in a kiss as he slipped his hand into her bodice and palmed her breast. She moaned under his lips as he filled his hand with her flesh, so hot and round and firm, and his thumb teased a nipple that was as hard as a blackberry.

Both of them were panting when he finally broke the kiss, and he barely restrained himself from rolling her into the backseat and tearing the gown off her altogether. Instead, he pulled away and watched the delicious process of Eve tucking herself back into her bodice, hiding her secrets from his avid gaze once more.

"You have the most beautiful breasts I've ever seen," he breathed, turning the key in the ignition. "I'm that kind of guy. Easily visually stimulated." He managed to get the car out of the driveway without hitting anything, and pressed the accelerator down once they were on the main road. "Do you ever go out without a bra?"

"Never." Her hand lay on his thigh, and his erection practically strained toward it, he wanted her to touch him so badly. But he'd probably run off the road if she did.

"Would you if I asked you to?"

"Maybe." A wicked smile teased the corners of her mouth.

"I want to see you tomorrow. For lunch or something. It's Saturday—anything. We won't tell a soul, and on Monday I'll deny it ever happened." She laughed, as if he'd confirmed something she already knew. "Wear a camisole for me and I'll spend the whole time watching the shape of you under the fabric. Saying things to make your nipples as hard as they are right now, so I can look at them."

"I'm so shocked," she murmured, her hand sliding down the inner slope of his thigh. "What will people think?" Her fingers brushed his aching erection, and he sucked a breath between his teeth.

"They'll think you're a beautiful, sexy woman," he got out, "and all the men will wish they were with you." He managed to brake just in time for a Stop sign. "And if you don't stop that, we're going to have an accident."

"You touched me," she pointed out.

"You weren't driving. And besides, you asked me to. Begged me, if I recall."

"I did, didn't I?" She pulled her hand back so its

burning warmth rested once again on his thigh, and she gave him a sideways glance. "But I was just saying out loud what you wanted."

"Damn right. Do I turn left or right here?" She pointed, and the car leaped forward. "Because there's nothing I want more right now than to kiss that dress right off you, inch by inch."

She did the shimmy with her shoulders again, and the bodice slid down so that it seemed only a miracle kept her nipples from popping out over the rim of the fabric. His entire body throbbed with anticipation.

"How do you do that?" He dragged his gaze back to the highway. In the distance he could see the lighted block of the hotel. Thank God.

"Faulty engineering. Keep your eyes on the road, Mr. Hayes." With a fingertip, her eyes on his face, she traced the top of the bodice. Teasing. Promising.

"I can't. Not when you're giving me a visual feast. And I'm about five seconds from orgasm just looking."

"At eighty miles an hour? Better slow down."

"I'm in a hurry. I want to get you up to my room before you come out of that dress again."

"Mmm," she crooned, her other hand moving stealthily to stroke his erection through his black dress pants. He shuddered with pleasure. "I could come in it."

"Not a chance. When you come, it'll be screaming, naked and on top of me." The speedometer edged up to eighty-five.

"Promises, promises."

Her hand felt so good. "Eve, please," he choked. "I

can't— I'm going to—" The tires chattered on the highway dots as he drifted into the next lane.

With a throaty chuckle, she pulled away and settled into the passenger's seat, both hands primly in her lap, and he steered the Lexus back into the middle of the lane.

Almost there.

Dimly, Mitch heard a jingling sound, but his senses were so overwhelmed with Eve that it barely registered. Until the second time. Then the third.

"That's my phone." She sounded as surprised as if she'd never heard it before, and fumbled in her clutch bag.

"Let it go. We're nearly there."

She glanced at the wafer-thin screen, then back at him, her eyes full of apology. "I can't. No matter how much I want to."

THE NUMBER WAS JENNA'S, and Eve knew she'd been scheduled to meet with Liza's attorney that day. The fact that it was nearly midnight made it even more necessary for her to answer.

"Yes?"

"Eve? Thank goodness. I thought it was going to roll to voice mail."

"What's up?" Her voice still sounded throaty, and the ricochet of desire through her veins distracted her— though she'd have to forego the distraction for a few minutes and concentrate.

"It's stupid—I'm so sorry, Eve. I probably woke you up."

"Yes, but not the way you think." The heat in her

blood dropped a couple of degrees back toward normal. "Take a moment if you need to."

"It's just dumb," Jenna repeated. "But you're so good at this kind of thing and I'm afraid I've messed up big-time."

Eve glanced at Mitch, who was concentrating on a left turn into the hotel's underground parking lot. "Did the negotiations not go well?"

"About what I expected. Kevin had his arguments, I had my counterarguments. It ended in a draw."

"Kevin?" Eve said carefully.

Jenna sighed. "Yes. Kevin Wade, Liza's attorney. Therein lies the problem."

"What problem? Is he incompetent? If so, that's good for us, right?"

Jenna laughed, a sound that conveyed more irony than humor. "No, he's not incompetent. I am. I'm massively attracted to him and I made the mistake of showing it."

Mitch pulled into a numbered spot and turned off the engine. But instead of making her feel rushed and guilty because he'd lost her attention, he seemed content to simply lounge against the driver's side door, watching her. As if whatever she did gave him pleasure.

Focus. Jenna needs you.

"Where are you now?" Eve asked.

"Sitting outside his condo complex. I—I agreed to come back here with him—to discuss the case further, mind—but he must have stopped somewhere because he's not here yet. I need you to talk me out of going in."

Eve had to laugh. "He probably stopped at the drugstore for a box of condoms. If you want to do this, we'll just ask Andersen Nadeau for a different attorney for the lawsuit, and you keep the station's business as usual."

"You're not helping."

"You don't need my help. You're what, thirty-one? Two? You didn't put in all those years in law school to let someone else make your decisions for you."

"I know," Jenna moaned. "But I tell you what, Eve, that man is hot. And what's more, he thinks I'm hot. I've been sitting here weighing my caseload against the fact that I haven't been in bed with a real man in months, and the caseload is losing."

Eve could certainly relate to that. "If we have to get another attorney assigned to the suit, we can. But I have to say, I really respect that brain of yours. If anyone can pull this off with sympathy and grace, it's you."

"Now you tell me."

"I'm not trying to argue for either side. Just telling you how I feel."

"I'll never be able to explain the switch to Marv Andersen." Jenna sounded as if she were trying to talk herself out of going into that condo. "I'd have to make something up, and I'm a terrible liar."

"If you don't go, it's not like it's forever," Eve reasoned. "Mr. Wade must be as aware of the ethics as you are. Maybe he'll wait until the case is over."

"We had such a good time at dinner, Eve," Jenna said in a rush. "He's so interesting to talk to, and then the whole will-we-or-won't-we thing just added this zing to the evening. I'm only supposed to be staying for a drink and another look at the brief, but I know as well as he does it won't end there."

Eve glanced again at Mitch, but he just grinned at her. Their situation wasn't that much different, was it? She was consorting with the enemy, too, though it wasn't likely she'd get into as much of a legal tangle over it as Jenna.

Men. They could really mess with a girl, couldn't they? Since when had sex and a career become so complicated?

Hmm. That might make a good segment for—

"Eve? Are you there?"

She dragged her gaze off Mitch's fly, where it had inexplicably landed, and gave her attention back to her attorney. "I'm here. I was just thinking."

"I have to go," Jenna said urgently. "Before he comes back. If I see him again I'll give in, and I don't want to do that. I want to see this case through."

"Good girl."

"I really appreciate you letting me talk through this."

"No problem. I know you'd do the same for me."

"So, where are you, anyway?" In the background, Eve heard keys jingle and an engine fire up.

"On my way home from the Atlanta Reads benefit at the Ashmere place." Well, it wasn't a lie. Technically she was between the benefit and home, which meant she was on her way there, right?

"Oh, yeah. I hope it was fun. Look, I've got to go. This is a stick shift and I need both hands."

"Take care."

"Bye, and thanks again."

Eve snapped the phone shut and tucked it into her bag. "Thanks for being patient," she said to Mitch.

The ghost of a smile was still playing around the corners of his mouth. "No problem. Sounds like we're not the only ones with a hot date."

"Isn't that the truth. Only I managed to talk her out of it."

One eyebrow rose. "Bit of a buzzkill, are you?"

Her body temperature was back to normal now. In fact, the skin on her bare arms and shoulders felt down-right cool from the air-conditioning, which he'd considerately kept running. "It was the right thing to do. If she'd stayed, it would have compromised her ethics in a business matter."

"Can't have that." He turned off the air, and silence fell. "Shall we go up?"

The moment of truth. Eve forced herself to relax her grip on her beaded handbag before she did some damage to it.

"I don't think so, Mitch. Up until five minutes ago, my answer would have been completely different, but—"

"But your friend's ethics problem might be yours, too?"

"I think you have to admit that it is," she said quietly, and paused. After leading him on all night, she owed him honesty after changing her mind. "If I go with you, it might change the way I look at CWB's proposal. And that wouldn't be fair. I have to think about what's best for the program, not only myself."

"Is that likely to happen?" he asked. "The one has nothing to do with the other."

The phrase triggered a memory of one of their shows from last year. They'd focused on the differences in the ways men and women process information. How much mileage had she and Nicole and Jane got from that? They'd all learned how much men tended to compartmentalize. Men—or at least the ones who had been guests on the show—seemed to have two boxes in their brains, one labeled Sex and one labeled Everything Else.

Clearly, for Mitch, this evening fell into the first box.

It had for her, too, for a couple of delirious, wonderful hours. But how long could she keep it there, particularly if, as he'd said, she'd be seeing him in her office on Monday, as determined as ever to buy her away from her friends? She couldn't just put a dividing line between "fantasy weekend" and "real life" and expect everything to stay neatly on either side of the line.

"We might not see it that way right now," she admitted, "but on Monday we will. And we'll probably be sorry." She felt the bullet shape of her cell phone under her fingers, through her bag. "Do you mind walking me to the lobby? There's a cab line out front."

"You're not taking a cab." He fired up the engine and fastened his seat belt once more. "I'll take you home."

She put a hand on his arm. "No, Mitch, a cab's fine. Really. I'm not far from here."

"In that case, it won't take us long." He backed out of the parking stall and she gave in.

"You don't plan on stalking me once you know where I live, do you?" she asked, directing him to turn left at the intersection.

"It's not a bad idea," he said, "but I believe we have

a date for tomorrow. This way, I can pick you up. Turn here?"

"The second right, then the first left. Were you serious about tomorrow?"

"Certainly." His sidelong glance tracked lazily down her body, reminding her vividly that he hadn't wanted her to wear underwear. "Breakfast, lunch, whatever you want. You could show me around. If you don't have plans, that is."

She couldn't have told him what her calendar said if her life depended on it. That hungry gaze sent a ripple of desire through her belly. And it reminded her of how very dangerous it was to spend any more time with this man than it took to say no and show him the door.

"The white bungalow, there," she managed to say. "Number 954."

He turned into her driveway and parked, looking over the front of her house. "Nice," he said. "Smaller than I would have expected for a celebrity. And the rambling roses over the door are a nice touch."

You could still invite him in, the treacherous voice of her desire whispered. *You could still have him, if that look a minute ago was any indication.*

"Thanks." She cleared her throat. "It used to be a carriage house for that mansion there." She pointed through the trees. "But it's big enough for me. Big houses are for big families…or big egos. None of which apply here."

He glanced at her. "You haven't answered my question."

"Which one was that?"

"Whether I can see you tomorrow." A dozen different answers crashed into one another in her mind, and he seemed to think that her hesitation meant she needed convincing. "Take pity on a Yankee, Eve," he said. "What am I going to do with myself for two days if you don't help me out?"

She was absolutely sure he'd have no problem finding something. The Braves were playing, there were concerts galore all over town, and at least two art exhibits were scheduled to open the next day.

"Come on," he wheedled. "Let's forget our job titles and the size of our in-boxes and do something fun, all right?"

Absolutely not. The more time she spent with him, the more difficult it would be to see him on Monday. The show came first. The words organized in her mind, she opened her mouth to say them.

"All right," she said. "But I'm wearing a bra."

5

THE WARMTH OF THE SUN on her eyelids woke Eve, telling her she'd forgotten to close the drapes before she'd gone to sleep the night before. No wonder. Her mind had been such a maelstrom of sex and ethics and work worries that it was a miracle she'd remembered to lock the front door.

But then, Mitch had been on the other side of it, sitting in the car with the engine running until she'd let herself inside and turned the porch light on and off. She hadn't locked him out. Oh, no. She'd locked herself in, away from him.

She'd done the right thing. Okay, so maybe it hadn't been so smart to agree to see him today, but after all, what could happen in broad daylight? Last night had been a combination of champagne, dancing and moonlight; that was it. Now that she'd had some sleep and could think rationally, it'd be easy to keep her distance.

In fact, she could practice saying no all day to get herself in shape for saying it again on Monday.

She'd just started a pot of coffee when the phone rang. And here he was. When he'd asked for her phone number as she was getting out of the car, she'd given it to him, figuring it was better that he call instead of driving over here. Maybe he'd be happy with a phone call. Maybe he'd reconsidered seeing her.

"Eve, it's Jane."

Eve took a moment to regroup. Jane, not Mitch. Well, that was a relief.

Wasn't it? "Hey, sweetie. I thought you were going to the benefit, but I didn't see you."

"No, we, uh, didn't make it out of the bedroom once I got my stockings on. Perry calls me his sexy librarian."

Eve smiled. At least someone was getting some action in the bedroom. If it couldn't be her, she was glad it was Jane. After all she'd been through, Jane deserved every minute of the happiness she'd found with Perry.

"Stockings and high heels will do it every time. So, what's up?"

Jane hesitated. "Can I talk to you?"

"Sure." She pulled out a kitchen chair and made herself comfortable while the coffee dripped. "I've got nothing but time." And while she was talking to Jane, Mitch couldn't get through. And if he couldn't get through, she could push off seeing him.

"Not over the phone. I'd rather talk in person."

A chill wriggled through Eve's stomach. "What's the matter?"

"Can't we—"

"Jane, you can't say something like that and not expect me to ask. What's going on? Are you okay? Did something happen?"

Jane sighed. "I'm fine, nothing happened. Relax. I've just been thinking, that's all."

"About what?" What could she possibly need a face-to-face for when they saw each other daily and talked all the time?

"I—I've been thinking about the future. About my place on the show, given all the rumors flying around the station about the networks coming to call."

For a second, Eve forgot to breathe. Her lungs constricted, and she took a deep breath. "I'm listening."

"Perry's won his lawsuit. Once we win ours, he and I can move anywhere we want. Travel. Do the things I've always wanted to do but never had the guts or the reason. Don't get me wrong—I'm yours for life if you want me, and I'd never leave the show just on a whim. But with the possibility of change in the future, I wanted to sound you out about it."

Eve squelched the urge to wail, *But you're my best friend! What about me?* With Jane, the facts worked best. If she could ground her argument in facts rather than emotion, she had a chance.

"Don't forget we haven't actually got the money yet. Wouldn't it be wiser to go on as usual until we have the checks in our hands?"

"If you're talking about the lawsuit, Liza has absolutely no grounds to stand on. The case will be thrown out."

"It hasn't yet, and how many hearings have we been to?" Eve asked. "It would be foolish to go into even more debt booking trips and buying land or whatever our dreams might be, when we may never see the money. Or at least, not for months or even years."

"Don't say that," Jane groaned.

"Let's look at reality." Ha, that was pretty clever. Use one of Jane's favorite expressions on her. "Until the lawsuit's settled, we need to go on as usual. And if the show goes on, it'll need you. I'm not setting foot in that studio without you to put my face on."

"Makeup artists are a dime a dozen," Jane said. "The minute the word gets out that the thought has even crossed my mind, the applicants will be lining up around the block along with the studio audience."

"Your usual artist might be a dime a dozen," Eve allowed, "but you're not. You gave me my signature look with that nifty Swiss foundation. And don't forget how valuable you are in the brainstorming department. Would we have done the 'High School Reunion Makeover' episode and broken a ratings record?"

"That was a lot of fun…"

Detecting signs of weakening resolve, Eve moved in for the kill. "And would Rosanne Horton have snagged the former quarterback she'd loved her whole life if not for you? I think not."

Jane chuckled. "Low blow, Best. She still writes to me, you know. I'm expecting baby pictures anytime now."

"She's grateful. And so am I. Please don't turn in your resignation just yet, okay? Let Jenna get the suit settled and then think about it."

Jane was silent, and Eve held her breath.

"All right. I'll tell Perry he's going to have to wait to go to Europe, and he should put his bankroll into a nice money market fund instead."

Relief washed over Eve in a cool wave. "Good plan. Have a great weekend. See you Monday."

"I'll make it up to him," Jane said wickedly. "Where's that other package of stockings?"

Laughing, Eve hung up. Then she poured herself a cup of coffee, splashed in some milk, and drank half of it down. A disaster, nipped in the bud. Not bad for first thing in the morning.

The truth was, she didn't know what she'd do without Jane's level head around the station. On some days, when a guest made impossible demands or dropped out without warning, or a sponsor was difficult, or even when Atlanta's heat index got too high, Eve would find Jane, close the door and vent until she was calm again. Inevitably, Jane would have a different angle Eve hadn't seen, or just a few words that would put everything in perspective again.

Facing the demands of live television without her oldest friend at her side was unthinkable. And not only Jane, but Cole and Zach and Nicole. What might they be planning? If the thought had crossed Jane's mind, it had certainly crossed the others', too.

Please don't let them all decide to resign at once, she begged the universe. *I can't handle it right now.*

As though it would give her strength, she topped up her coffee and padded into the bathroom for a shower. When she came out, a light blinked on the answering machine.

"Hey, Eve, it's Mitch." Eve sucked in a breath at the sound of that voice, pitched at an intimate baritone, as if he were right beside her. "Just wanted to call and say how much I enjoyed last night, and to see how you were this morning. Give me a call on my cell. I'm still up for breakfast—or lunch—if you are." He left his number and rang off.

At least he didn't want to resign.

Just the opposite. He seemed to want to sign up for all kinds of things—including the positions of dealmaker and lover. Too bad the latter came as part of the former. Why couldn't she have met him at the benefit the way she might meet any other man, as a stranger with no strings attached? But if she did what her body had been moaning for since last night, she'd never be sure whether he wanted her in bed with him—or with the network.

She refilled her coffee cup and leaned on the counter, gazing at the answering machine and the single digit on the display. Common sense told her to erase the message and pretend she'd been so busy all weekend she'd forgotten to listen to it—and forgotten her promise to see him today. By Monday, she'd have squelched this urge to play it again, just to hear that intimate timbre in his voice. By Monday, she'd have distanced herself from the need to rip her clothes off and bare herself to that hot gaze, the memory of which was even now making her nipples peak under the tank top she'd put on after her shower.

Jane would advise her to do something sensible, like eat a healthy breakfast and then weed the garden before it got too hot. She could do two things at once—restore some order to the tangle of vegetation back there, and not hear the phone if it rang again.

But Jane wasn't here. She was busy seducing Perry. And how fair was that?

MITCH HAD BARELY hung up the phone after leaving his message for Eve, when it rang again. He must have just missed her.

"Hey," he said in his most welcoming tone.

"Hey, yourself," Nelson Berg responded. "Something tells me it wasn't me you were expecting."

Mitch's vision of a tousled Eve lying on embroidered white sheets, her fingers caressing the phone as she spoke to him, vanished in a wrench of disappointment. "Uh, no. I mean, not that I'm not glad to hear from you."

"Spare me the bull. So, how are you doing?"

Mitch knew Nelson well enough not to assume this was an inquiry after his health. Nelson never wasted precious time on pleasantries, especially when there was a deal in the works.

"I met with Eve Best in her office yesterday, late. I made her the offer and she turned it down."

Nelson sighed. "Why would she do that? It was a fair offer."

"She didn't give a reason."

"Huh? She had to have one."

"She just said no. She had an appointment to go to and left." He didn't mention that he'd been the one to leave, as flustered and dazzled as a schoolboy.

"Well, shit, Hayes, you can't let it go at that."

"I know. I've already—"

"Find out what her reasons are and get her past them. They can't be anything that six million bucks won't cure."

Mitch wasn't so sure of that. "Money isn't going to be the best argument here, I'm afraid."

"What do you—" Nelson stopped. "Oh yeah. The lottery. So if it isn't money it has to be something else. Find out what it is and work on it. When are you seeing her next?"

"I saw her last night, socially, and she agreed to see me this morning."

"Did she, now?" Nelson sounded gratified, as if a balky student had finally done something right. "That's good. I'm glad you're following my instructions to the letter. So, tell me, does she have as much appeal in person as she does on camera?"

Does she ever. And then some.

"Yes. And she works it. The event last night was a fund-raiser, and she walked in there like a star. She'll be a huge draw publicitywise."

"All the better. We can use some big guns on the talk shows and the publicity circuit, drumming up support for the network. Not to mention high-level meetings with advertisers. Make sure she knows that'll still be part of her job, not just sitting pretty in the studio."

"Sure."

"Call me right away when you get her commitment. I want this wrapped up by Wednesday at the latest. And then I'm going to let all the other networks know we scooped them."

Mitch frowned. Wednesday? No way could he pull a deal of this size off in that short a time. Did Nelson have something else to prove—something that involved saving face and putting one over on the competition?

If so, why hadn't he come down here to woo Eve Best himself? Why send Mitch? But these were questions he knew Nelson wouldn't answer. The guy only knew how to bark orders and bully people into giving him what he wanted. He didn't share his motivations or the confidences of the stuffed shirts on the executive team. Nelson was old-school, even though he was only ten years or so older than Mitch himself.

"Wednesday." No human could make that deadline, but he'd ask forgiveness when he got there. And there was something else bugging him. "What did you mean a minute ago when you said I was following your instructions? When have I not?"

"I told you to romance the socks off her. Probably not a very difficult job, eh?"

Mitch frowned. The words held an unpleasant aftertaste. Or was he being too sensitive where Eve was concerned? "She's being a good Southern hostess and showing me around."

The details of last night would never cross his lips to anyone, much less his boss. And the simple fact that Nelson assumed any contact with Eve would be to further their success at the deal made Mitch feel...less, somehow. Tainted. This electric attraction between the two of them had nothing to do with what they did for a living. It was bigger than that. The problem was, he had to keep his feelings to himself, no matter what he wanted personally.

Not that he'd ever say a word about them to Nelson.

"Look, I have to go," he said. "I left a message for her to call me a few minutes ago. She could be trying to get through."

That finally got Nelson off the phone, and Mitch hung up with a sense of relief. No matter what he felt about Nelson, or Eve, for that matter, of course he had a job to do. Convincing Eve to sign was his top priority—one he needed to remember if he saw her again this morning. He had to do his best not to see her as a desirable, sensual woman who could bring his entire body to attention simply by walking past him.

No, he had to shut down his emotions and look at her as a business entity. A package that CWB wanted. His future at the network depended on his ability to bring that package home—by Wednesday.

And what a package she was—one he had nearly unwrapped last night. Could anything be sexier than Eve Best leaning in for a kiss, her bodice slipping down to reveal lush curves and her voice husky in his ear? As the memory washed through his mind, his body stiffened in response.

So much for shutting down.

The phone next to the bed rang, and the vision in his head snapped off as suddenly as if someone had changed the channel. With a groan, he picked it up. It was probably Nelson, with one last order to give him. "Hello?"

"Hi, it's Eve."

The voice brought back the vision in full force. "Hey," he said softly. "I was just thinking about you."

"Sorry I missed your call. I was in the shower."

A picture of wet skin, of water running in rivulets between her breasts and down her belly, leaped onto the big screen in his mind. In close-up.

"Mitch?"

He had to turn off the film, or he'd never be able to carry on a civilized conversation. "I'm here. Sorry. I thought there was a knock at the door."

"Do you want me to hold while you check?"

"No, no. It was probably someone going past with

a suitcase." He was such a lousy liar. "So, does this mean we're on for breakfast?"

"I know I said yes last night, but I really can't. I'm sorry. I have a ton of things to do."

"Like what?"

He really was interested in the details of her life, but as soon as the words were out, he realized how they must sound.

"Well, I have to work on Monday's script, and go grocery shopping, and try to hack my way through the jungle in my backyard, and—"

"Don't you ever relax on the weekend?"

"That *is* relaxation. Well, except for the script."

"Do it tomorrow."

"I have Tuesday's script to work on tomorrow, and some preliminary work to do on this communications specialist we're bringing in on Thursday. Then I have to go over to North Point Mall and try to find my cousin's four-year-old a birthday present. I'm invited to my aunt and uncle's place tonight for dinner and the party." She paused. "That's way too much information, isn't it?"

"Boy or girl?"

"Boy."

"Ah. He'll love anything to do with dinosaurs or Spider-Man."

"How do you know?"

"My sister's kids are that age. Two boys and a girl. Brandon knows the Latin names of every dinosaur that ever lived, and a few that are cartoon characters, as well."

Her laugh made his breath hitch. What was it about this woman that affected him this way? Was he that long overdue for sex and therefore more susceptible than usual? Or did she charm everyone like this?

"Duly noted," she said. "That should simplify things."

An idea whisked into his mind. "I could come along. Offer some suggestions. Dinosaurs can get out of hand in a hurry without the help of an expert." And while he was at it, he could pitch her again.

"You seriously don't want to go to the mall with me." Her voice filled with disbelief, though laughter lurked in the back of it. "A big network exec like you? Don't you have important stuff to do? Deals to nail down? People to see?"

"I do," he said. "One deal in particular is very important to me, but I refuse to let it interfere with my weekend."

She paused, as though this were sinking in. "I see. So today and tomorrow are a deal-free zone? The subject won't come up, even in passing?"

"Will you push me into the fountain by the food court if it does?"

"I don't think there is a fountain, but probably." The laughter bubbled closer to the surface now, and his whole being seemed to warm with it.

"I'll take the risk. So how about you put the garden off until tomorrow, and we hit the mall today? Do the script this morning, and I'll pick you up after lunch."

"What about breakfast?"

"I'll get some here. If we bag our 'saur, we can celebrate with a victory drink."

She was laughing openly now. "Deal. Pick me up around two. I'll be done with the script by then if I concentrate."

He agreed and rang off, her laughter still tickling his mind, giving him as much pleasure as her fingers might on his skin.

She might be able to find some powers of concentration. But the prospect of spending the afternoon with her had shot his straight to hell.

6

PROMPTLY AT TWO, the doorbell rang and Eve opened the door to find Mitch hunched awkwardly on the porch under the heavy cover of the rambling roses.

"You might consider trimming these things," he suggested by way of greeting. "I think one of them just bit me."

Eve waved him inside. "They don't have thorns. And I keep them that way to remind myself not to let my head swell. You know, with success. They remind me to stay humble."

Her house wasn't that big—a dining room and kitchen on the left of the hall, and a parlor and family room on the right, the latter of which had become her office over the past three years. The bathroom and two bedrooms were at the back, but weren't visible from where he stood.

"I can't imagine you having problems with that," he said. "Nice place."

"Thanks." She waved him into the parlor. "The furniture is from my aunt and uncle's attic, mostly. The coffee table was my mom's. My grandmother in Florida died a year and a half ago, and I got some of her pieces, too, like that sideboard."

"So you have pieces of your family with you." His tone was abstract, as if his situation were completely the opposite. "And the piano?" He opened the lid and touched a key with one long finger.

Eve looked away. "My dad's. He was a big fan of Pinetop Perkins and the old boogie-woogie piano players. My mom used to keep plants on top of it and he could really make them dance once he got going."

Sure enough, ancient water rings were etched into the finish. Mitch pulled out the bench and sat. "Do you mind?"

"Not a bit. It's probably out of tune, though."

"Boogie, huh? I wonder if anyone remembers where that word came from." He rolled out a walking bass with his left hand.

She laughed, a huff of amazement. "I thought you said you were a trumpet player."

He began to pick out notes with the right hand. "I started on the piano when I was a kid. Mom was a music teacher. I haven't done this in a while. I think I've lost my knack."

"Here, shove over." Eve sat down on the other half of the piano bench and glanced at his bass notes to see the key. The rhythms her dad had pounded out on this very spinet seemed to be embedded in it still—or maybe they were just in her memory. She found a melody she'd learned as a kid and began to embellish it.

Mitch's bass was as steady as a rock, if you didn't count the flourishes of syncopation that made her shoulders sway with the rhythm, and suggested skipped beats and notes of her own.

Eve had had years of piano lessons when she'd lived with Nana, who had believed firmly that her dad's talent slept inside her somewhere, all evidence to the contrary. In about her fifth year, she'd got the hang of it and the piano became pleasure, not work. She'd never played in a band, though, or any kind of ensemble that would prepare her for the sheer organic sensuality of making music with another person.

Melody and bass, rhythm and counterpoint. Line building on line, notes forming chords forming song. Two people bringing their experience together to create something entirely new and different.

The way they might when they made love.

Eve lost her concentration and a straightforward diminished A fumbled into discord. Mitch's rhythm faltered and stopped.

"Whoa," she said, summoning a grin and sliding off the bench. "Lost it. I guess I need more practice."

"Sounded pretty good to me." He slid off the bench, too, and closed the lid carefully over the ivories. "But then, I imagine there isn't much you don't do well."

Eve mumbled something appropriately self-deprecating and headed down the hall to get her handbag. It wasn't fair. The relationship gods must hate her. Here she was in a career that depended on the whole world of relationships for its bread and butter. She'd met a gorgeous man who seemed to be as attracted to her as she was to him, and who had voluntarily suggested going to a mall without being threatened with blackmail first.

Why did he have to be the one man she had to hold at arm's length? In the practical light of common day, she reflected from the safety of her bedroom, she'd been insane to behave the way she had last night. Nana would be so—not shocked, because Eve couldn't imagine much shocking her—but disappointed. And she'd always hated disappointing Nana. That sad look, that biting of the lip that meant she could be giving the young Eve an earful but was holding it back so as not to hurt…oh, yeah. Very effective. She could have used a shot of Nana last night.

Eve glanced at her tank top and jeans in the mirror, and pulled a gauze tunic off its hanger and slipped it on overtop. There. Much better. Some comfortable sandals in matching green, a green wallet-on-a-string, and she was ready to go.

If only Mitch wasn't such good company.

As they cruised toy stores, movie tie-in stores and educational stores in search of the perfect dinosaur for four-year-old Christopher, she kept things deliberately on a friendly business-lunch footing. But by the time they'd begun triangulating the mall's second level for a renewed attack, she'd given up the pretense. How was a girl supposed to keep her distance when he insisted on cracking jokes about passersby or things in the windows? How was she supposed to put last night out of her head when every time she turned suddenly, she caught him watching her? Which wasn't a problem—lots of people watched her. So far three women had come up and asked for her autograph, in fact.

This was the gaze of a man silently undressing a woman in his mind. Not just undressing, either. He was making love to her behind that innocent, bland gaze, she was sure of it.

Luckily they found the perfect dinosaur in a nature store, and she led the way out of the mall with a sense of relief. She needed to go home and back to reality, and forget he was even in Atlanta, wanting her.

Just the way she wanted him.

No, no. She couldn't let her thoughts wander that way. It wasn't good for her peace of mind—and it certainly wasn't good for *Just Between Us*.

"It's four o'clock." Mitch shook his sleeve down over his watch. "I vote for lunch."

Eve arranged her face in a regretful expression— which didn't take much. "I can't. I really need to get home and get ready to go to dinner. And I should look at that script one more time."

"Creativity never came on an empty stomach." He grinned, and her resolve wavered, then straightened up.

"Then where do all the starving artists come from?" she quipped. "I appreciate your helping me out, Mitch. I now know as much about toy dinosaurs as I'll need to know for the rest of my life. It was good of you to take the time."

"Come on." His long stride kept pace with hers effortlessly as they headed back to his car. "My hotel's across the parking lot. Let me treat you to lunch. Or at least a snack before your dinner. Remember, you agreed."

"I agreed to breakfast. Maybe it's just as well we're out of time."

He put a hand on her arm to slow her down. "What does that mean?"

"Let's talk about it somewhere less public, okay?"

She could tell he was holding back what he wanted to say with an effort that lasted through the parking garage, down the street and all the way back to her house. But as soon as she got out and retrieved her package from the backseat, he closed his door with the sound of finality.

"This is less public, wouldn't you say?"

She opened the front door and dropped the package and her green bag in the hall, then turned in the doorway to face him. Even hunched under the roses, he looked completely masculine and, if not comfortable, then at least in command of himself.

Words failed her. How could she tell him she didn't want to see him socially when she'd only be lying to herself—and him?

"May I come in?"

"No. If I had any sense, I'd ask you to go back to your hotel and book an earlier flight home to New York."

"You know I'm not going to do that."

"You should. There's no reason to stay here."

"I can think of one. And I'd like to talk about it somewhere other than on your doorstep. A beetle just dropped down the back of my neck."

How could she chase away a guy who made her smile every five minutes? She turned her head so he wouldn't see it flickering at the corners of her lips, and stepped back. "Fine. But only for a few minutes."

He closed the door behind him and began to unfasten the buttons of his shirt. Her mouth dropped open.

One button. Two. Three.

What was this? Did he think an invitation to talk for a few minutes was some kind of thinly disguised come-on? Not that she was complaining about the view, but a girl had her principles.

Four, five. Was he—was he—

Oh, my.

He peeled off the shirt and her jaw felt as though it had become unhinged. Along with her mind.

Because, naked to the waist, Mitchell Hayes was just about the most beautiful thing she'd ever seen. Muscle flexed and moved under smooth, tanned skin as he shook out his shirt. There wasn't an ounce of extra fat anywhere. A broad chest narrowed to a finely honed set of abs, and dark, curly hair arrowed down and disappeared into the waistband of his jeans.

"There you are, you little rascal." He knelt and scooped up the black beetle skittering across the tile of the entryway, then opened the door and tossed it back into the thicket of roses.

Breathe. Take a breath. Good. Now, close your mouth and behave as if everything is normal.

Turning, he buttoned up his shirt and tucked the tails into his jeans as though nothing had happened.

Look away from the jeans.

"Eve, you okay?" He bent sideways to look into her face.

"Yes." She reached for something sensible to say. Should she apologize? "It's not often that my visitors strip when they walk in, that's all."

"If I'm going to have someone walking on my back, I'd rather she didn't have six legs." He paused. "And I find that very hard to believe. I bet any boyfriend of yours strips when he hits the door."

"I bet he doesn't," she batted back. "Or at least, if he existed, he wouldn't. I'm sorry about the banzai attack. Usually my insect life is better behaved."

"You're kidding me."

"No. Once in a while the moths come in if I leave the porch light on, and the june bugs are awful, but—"

"I didn't mean the bugs, I meant the boyfriend."

The refrigerator door made a very effective shield. The last thing she needed was for him to see the color wash into her face. "I have a chunk of Brie and some grapes here. If you were hungry before, you're probably starving now."

Oops. Hadn't she just said he'd get a few minutes and then he had to go? *Now, see, that's what you get for gawking at his abs. He's completely scrambled your brain.*

"And you're avoiding a really interesting topic."

She pulled out some celery and a plastic tub of guacamole. She had chips in the pantry, and half a salami. Would that be enough? All that muscle was probably the result of downing slabs of roast beef. "Are you kidding? You just took off your clothes in my foyer. It's impossible to avoid you."

"So let me get this straight. You're the relationship guru, the most desirable woman in Atlanta, the subject of several fan sites—I do my homework, don't look at me like that—and you don't think your man would be racing to get naked for you?"

"Maybe," she said as coolly as she could. She had

fan sites? "But I don't have time for a relationship, as I think I made clear."

"That's plain wrong," he said.

She shrugged. "It's reality."

He crossed his arms over his chest and leaned a hip on the end of the breakfast bar. "Leaving time out of it, do you *want* one?"

Her knife sliced into the salami with precision. "Of course. But it's pretty hard to ask a man to play second fiddle to the show. I mean, he'd have to. I work sixteen hours a day."

"You've just never met anyone who could make you rearrange your priorities, that's all."

Was that a glint of challenge in his eyes? "Oh, and you think you're the man who can do it?"

Certainly he could. If a man like Mitch were waiting at the studio door, she'd say damn the calendar and hit the stairs at a run. Not that she'd ever say that to him.

"Why not? Hypothetically speaking." The challenge was now complicated by humor. And—face it—temptation.

"I don't even have to speak hypothetically." She put the Brie on a plate and slipped it into the oven to warm, then picked up the knife again. "I'm afraid you've been bumped off the candidate list because of who you are."

"Didn't we agree that I was simply an honest guy from New Mexico?"

"That was last night." A subject she did not want to bring up. "The simple fact is that even seeing you like this compromises me professionally. I don't even know why I'm making you a snack."

"Because you're a well-brought-up Southern girl?"

"That wouldn't cut it with Dan Phillips. He owns CATL-TV and our production company. Mitch, I owe him a lot, including my loyalty. If it wasn't for him and Cole having so much faith in me, I'd still be talking about overnight lows and how the rain is affecting the commute for four and a half minutes every hour."

"That's right. You used to be the weathergirl. I saw a picture on one of those fan sites I mentioned. You looked to be fresh out of college."

"I was. So you can see that every minute we spend together makes it look like I'm consorting with the enemy. So to speak."

"You can consort with whomever you like on your time off," he pointed out.

"Most business consorting would happen in a meeting with you in my office, where everything is aboveboard. Not in my kitchen or—" *my bedroom* "—or anywhere else. I feel like I'm sneaking around on Dan behind his back."

"Okay, I can see that. But you have to admit, this way of consorting is more fun."

"Sure it is. But I'm a realist, and the reality is that CWB wants to take me away from CATL-TV. The station's done a lot for me. I can't just run out on them the moment the going gets good."

"CWB can do a lot more for you," Mitch said. "Take you national. Give the show a wider scope. Bigger production values. More audience reach."

"Yes, so you said in our meeting. Which, I might point out, this is not."

It was a sight better than talking about honest bodies and relationships, though. At least when they talked business, she had open-and-shut answers. When it came to Mitch and anything personal, she was very much afraid she didn't have answers of any kind.

"Are you done torturing that salami?" He leaned over the counter and grimaced. "If I didn't know better, I'd say you had some Freudian prejudice against the subject of relationships."

"Or symbols of male power," she said sweetly. "But I wouldn't read anything into it. It's a snack. A short one. Because I still have my to-do list waiting for me."

Hands on hips, he looked over her kitchen, taking in the white tile, the skylight, the basket of onions and garlic on the granite counter. Her answering machine sat next to it.

"You have a message."

She licked salami flavor off her index finger and punched the button. The man had strummed pleasure from her body the night before. He'd helped her find a dinosaur. It was a little late to worry about whether he should listen to her personal messages.

"Eve, honey, this is Grandmother Charlotte," her dad's mother said. If the Queen Mother had been brought up in the fields of Georgia, she would have looked and sounded like Charlotte Best. Eve straightened at the sound of her soft vowels, as if she'd reminded her about her posture. "I'm looking forward to seeing you tonight at Roy's. Do bring along an escort if you'd like to." Her grandmother laughed, and Eve's stomach sank. "I know it's hard, but choose one of your collection to introduce to your family. Bye-bye."

Eve resisted the urge to bang her head against the nearest cupboard door. Could there be anything more intimidating than a Southern lady determined to get her eldest, most successful granddaughter married off?

When Eve glanced at Mitch, his eyes were dancing. "I take it your grandmother is deluded about your social life?"

She picked up the knife again and held the salami down as if it were going to escape. "In her day, the aim of a girl's life was to get married. She knows I'm not like that. She knows how busy I am."

"I don't think it's about being busy. I think you're just afraid. Of getting involved. Of me. Of what could happen if we really got together."

The knife thwacked through the last of the salami and hit the cutting board with a clack. Lucky thing her fingers hadn't been in the way. "A woman who's learned as much about men as I have can't be afraid of lil' ol' you." She mimicked Charlotte's accent.

"Prove it."

"How would you suggest I do that?" She licked her fingers, deliberately goading him. She knew exactly what he'd say. That he wanted to take her to bed. And then she'd tell him—

"Let me be your date tonight. Your grandmother would still be deluded, but at least she'd be happy."

Eve froze, staring at him, one finger still in her

mouth. Then she drew it out slowly, and his gaze dropped to it as though it were a magnet.

"I watched the 'Meet the Family, Pass the Test' episode," he said, and pure challenge flavored that grin. "Or didn't you mean what you said in your closing monologue?"

"What, that any man who'd subject himself to that voluntarily was a keeper?"

"Exactly. I dare you."

She lifted her chin. "You've got a deal, Mr. Hayes." She offered him the plate. "Salami?"

7

"SUGAR, YOU LOOK like one of my favorite actors."

Eve held her breath as her grandmother allowed Mitch to take her hand in his and squeeze her fingers. This was never going to work. No one had ever put anything over on Charlotte Best in Eve's lifetime. The woman had gone from riches to rags and back to riches again, and what she didn't know about the stock market, gardening and human nature wasn't worth knowing.

Eve couldn't possibly pass off Mitch as a date or even a serious boyfriend. In fact, they'd agreed that the truth was probably the best strategy. Charlotte would see right through anything else.

"And you look like one of my favorite actresses," Mitch told her. "But Helen Hayes only played women like you. She wasn't the real thing."

Charlotte chuckled and glanced at Eve. "You'll let him sit beside me at dinner, won't you, baby doll?"

Not on your life, sugar pie. "Now, Grandmother, no stealing my date."

Charlotte laughed again and patted Mitch's sleeve. "Mr. Hayes, this is my son Roy, and his wife Anne."

Mitch shook hands with his host and hostess. "I saw

you folks at the Ashmere benefit last night, but we didn't speak."

"No wonder," Aunt Anne said with a smile. "You spent the evening dancing with Eve—not that I blame her."

"Did you, now?" Charlotte said with interest. "The whole evening?"

"Practically. She—"

"Are Karen and John and the kids here yet?" Eve asked hastily. "I have Christopher's gift in the car."

"Not yet, but I'm expecting them any minute." Anne took their coats. "Why don't you show Mitch around? Roy, that roast needs to be carved before it's as tough as an old boot. Mama, would you like a cocktail before dinner?"

With the skill of a longtime hostess, Anne shepherded them out of the foyer until they were, Eve had no doubt, exactly where she wanted them.

Not that that was a bad thing.

She didn't mind having several rooms between Mitch and her grandmother's sharp gaze. Not to mention her sharp tongue. Charlotte figured she was too old to filter her comments through any screen but politeness. Other than that, the family had learned to expect just about anything.

They walked into the living room and Mitch looked around with a soundless whistle. "Is this how old money lives?" he asked in a low voice.

"No, this is how a developer lives," she murmured. "We might be an old family, but the money is long gone. My great-grandpa managed to lose it somehow. My grandmother went from having servants and a big mansion to living over a shop in genteel poverty. But Uncle Roy has always been smart about money. They don't want for much."

"I can see that."

"See what?"

Eve turned as Charlotte came in from the dining room, a pink martini in hand. "Can I offer you one of these, darlin'?"

"No, thanks, Grandmother. I'll have wine with dinner."

"The same," Mitch said.

"Good." Charlotte sipped it with satisfaction while Mitch studied the pictures on the walls.

"Mr. Best has a high regard for family," he observed. "I'm assuming these are all relatives, right?"

"Understatement of the year," Eve murmured. "There's a reason the walls are all painted white."

The ceilings in the house were high, which meant there was a good ten feet of wall space on which to hang more pictures than anyone should see outside of a gallery. When she'd first moved here, Eve had wondered how Anne could stand it, but then she'd realized there were as many from her side. A cluster of their immediate family hung over the sofa. Portraits marched up the wall next to the staircase, forming their own staircase pattern up to the second floor. There were black-and-white pictures on either side of the windows, and over the sideboard, and flanking the wall unit that housed a flat-screen television.

"There's nothing wrong with having a little pride in one's heritage," Charlotte said.

"Does he know who all these people are?" Mitch asked.

"We all do, young man. They're our family. In fact, if you'd like to—"

"Grandmother, I'm sure Mitch doesn't want to be introduced to every person in the room," Eve put in.

"That's the second time you've interrupted," her grandmother informed her crisply. "Where are your manners?"

Eve blinked. "I'm sorry."

"As I was saying, Bests have been in these parts for nearly a hundred and fifty years. It's quite natural that Roy would want to preserve as many reminders of where he comes from as he can. Of where *you* come from, lovey doll." She looked at Eve over the rim of her glass. "I look forward to the day when I can tell your children the stories attached to these pictures."

She was not going to get into *that* discussion with Mitch standing there.

"Do you like children, Mr. Hayes?"

Oh, God. Somebody stop her.

"I have to confess I haven't given it much thought. I have nieces and nephews, but I don't see them very often."

"Eve is going to have beautiful children," Charlotte said with satisfaction. "Roy's eldest girl married young, only eighteen, and hers are lovely. You'll see them when they *get* here. That Christopher reminds me of Roy when he was a boy."

"Grandmother," Eve said desperately, "I'm going to show Mitch the upstairs."

"Don't get up to any monkey business," Charlotte warned. "Your cousins will be here any minute."

It took the entire trip up the staircase under the watchful eyes of people in top hats and crinolines before the scalding blush faded from Eve's cheeks. "I'm sorry about that," she said to Mitch. "She's a handful. Says what she wants when she wants."

"Nothing wrong with that. If, as you say, she lost everything, it's natural she'd value what she's got left— her family. And their pictures."

"I meant about the monkey business. Honestly, I think she thinks I'm still thirteen and playing spin the bottle."

He grinned and pulled her into one of the bedrooms. "You have a problem with spin the bottle? Because let me tell you, you are amazingly kissable when you blush like that. You can spin in my direction anytime."

"I am not blushing."

"Are so." With the pad of his thumb, he brushed the arch of her cheekbone. "Right here." He touched the other cheek. "And here."

"Why are you doing this?" she whispered.

"You took me up on a dare."

"We agreed. We can't go down there and pretend to be a couple." His touch on her face was mesmerizing. In spite of herself, anticipation built as his fingers skimmed her jaw. "They'll see right through it. Especially Grandmother."

"Who's pretending?" he breathed, and kissed her.

And there they were, right back under the ivy at the benefit. His mouth, so soft and yet so assured, coaxed hers open as she allowed the dammed-up desire that had been cooking inside her all day to burst free. She melted against him and slid her arms around his neck, pulling him closer, hauling him against her so that his big, hot body was fused to hers.

It was only for a moment. In just a moment she'd stop kissing him, stop falling into this fog of need that seemed to blow up between them and blot out reality.

Dimly, she was aware of noise below, but her senses were so filled with the scent of Mitch as his temperature rose, with the touch of his hands as they slid urgently down her back, with the taste of his lips and how they seemed to stoke the fire deep inside—

"Eve!"

Something small and hard rammed into her legs like a freight train and she gasped, jerking out of Mitch's arms. Stupidly, she stared at the dark-haired boy wrapping her leg in a hug.

"Eve, it's my birthday! Did you bring me a present?"

Mitch stepped back and sanity flooded in. Behind him, Emily, Eve's cousin and Roy's youngest daughter, hung in the doorway with the earphones of her iPod around her neck. She looked as embarrassed as Eve felt.

"I couldn't stop him," Emily said. "He came barreling into my room and then saw you guys across the hall."

She hadn't even noticed that Emily had been in her room. What if she and Mitch had gotten carried away, as they always seemed to do whenever they let themselves be alone together? Both Emily and Christopher might have gotten an eyeful that would have warped them for life.

Chris jumped up and down. "Present, present, present—"

"All right, all right, little man," Mitch said as if he'd

known the boy all his life. "The present's in the car. I'll get it. And happy birthday, by the way."

Eve hugged Emily and followed Mitch and Chris downstairs. Now all she had to do was figure out how to keep the kid quiet—or at least distracted. Because what he'd interrupted certainly qualified as "monkey business."

IN FORTY HOURS of digital TV footage, Mitch had not seen Eve as uncomfortable as she was now. She sat opposite him at a table laid out as artistically as a painting—Anne Best's work. The lady might not be whipping out fouettés in *Swan Lake* any longer, but she sure knew how to bring art into daily life.

It was too bad that the whole scene reminded him of one of the photographs behind him on the wall—beautifully posed, with no indication of the emotion rolling around underneath.

"So, Mr. Hayes, where did you meet our Eve?" Charlotte Best asked after neatly cutting up her slab of roast beef.

"At the station," he replied. "I was there on business."

"What kind of business?"

How to put this without giving away too much? "I work for a network. We think her show can reach a wider audience, so I had some proposals for her."

Emily snickered, and her mother frowned at her across two place settings.

"How long ago was this? Since we saw you at the benefit last night, I'm assuming it was before that."

"That afternoon, in fact," he said, just as Eve kicked him under the table.

"You only met yesterday?" Charlotte's plucked eyebrows rose. "My, my. What a fast worker you are."

"He was *kissing* her," Christopher said around a mouthful of mashed potatoes. "Gross."

"Chris!" His mother, who had been introduced to Mitch as Karen, tried to hush him.

"Well, he was," Chris said.

"You don't need to point it out," Karen's husband, whose name Mitch had forgotten, told him. "Eve might not have thought it was gross."

"I certainly wouldn't have," Charlotte mused. "The next best thing to Pierce Brosnan."

"Mother!" Roy looked up from his own plate. "You're embarrassing our guest."

"Am I embarrassing you?" Charlotte looked at Mitch, and he lost control of the grin twitching at the corners of his lips.

"Not at all."

"You're embarrassing *me*," Anne informed them. "Can we direct the conversation away from Eve, please? She doesn't need to be in the spotlight when she's with her own family."

Mitch shot a glance at Anne. The words were measured and considerate, but with all that stripped away, what lay underneath? Could this elegant woman be jealous? Of what? As far as he could tell, her life wasn't tied all that tightly to Eve's.

"She isn't in the spotlight," Charlotte said in a tone as crisp as the baby romaine leaves she speared with her fork. "I was merely trying to get a rise out of her young man. No need to be embarrassed, Anne."

"Mama, please. Can we discuss something else?"

"I think Eve's career is worthy of discussion. I hardly ever get to see the girl. So Eve, are you going to take Mr. Hayes up on his proposals? The ones relating to business, of course."

"I can't talk about that here, Grandmother."

"Why on earth not? We're your family, and obviously you've talked about it with Mr. Hayes."

"As you might expect, any negotiations about the show are confidential."

"It's not likely we'll say anything, is it? Roy's got no connections to television, and Anne never talks about you anyway. Silent as the grave, that girl. No fun at all."

Mitch almost felt sorry for Anne Best. She sat so straight in the ladder-back chair that you could draw the proverbial ballerina's line from her earlobe to her hipbone.

"Just because some of us don't believe in gossip—" Anne murmured against her wineglass.

"Bosh," Charlotte snorted. "You like a good gossip as well as any of us. But I suppose we should be grateful that someone gives us an example of discretion to follow."

"I'm discreet, Grandmother," Emily said. "I never talk about Eve or her show, even though all the kids at school know I'm related."

"I should hope not," Anne said. "Half of what goes on in that show should be rated NC-17."

"What?" Eve choked on a green bean, and Mitch clapped her on the back. "You can't watch it anyway. It comes on before you get home from school."

"I have TiVo," Emily informed her smugly. "I tape it every day."

"You do?" her mother asked.

"Plus they post the episodes on YouTube, so if I forget I can watch them there."

"Emily, I hardly think that rainbow parties and finding out if your man is a keeper are the kinds of things you should be watching."

"Why not?" Charlotte wondered aloud. "I'm sure the halls of the junior high ring with exactly that kind of thing."

"Emily," Eve said, her face pale, "maybe you should consider your mom's feelings and watch something else."

"Why? I'm fourteen. It's a little late for the parental guidance now, and rainbow parties are so yesterday. Besides, you're my cousin. I learn all kinds of things from you."

Silence.

Mitch shifted in his seat and watched Anne. Half of him wanted to get Eve's coat and hustle her into the car. Half of him was fascinated by the veneer of politeness cracking over what was obviously a very sore subject.

"You can ask your mom and dad if you want to know about the things we talk about on the show," Eve said quietly.

"At least you talk about them," the girl retorted. "Mom and Dad don't talk about *anything*. Except what's for dinner and who's who in all these dumb pictures. Not about relationships and boys and stuff that's important."

"Emily, that's not true. And that's enough out of you. You're being very rude," admonished her mother.

"Now I can't talk to my own cousin?" Emily threw her napkin down. "First you want me to stop watching her show, and now you want me to stop talking to her?"

"That's not what I said."

Mitch could see that Roy was hanging on to his patience for the sake of his guests. "Please sit down and apologize."

"I didn't do anything except tell the truth."

"You have no idea what the truth even means," Anne snapped. Then she took a deep breath and looked at Mitch. "Can I offer you some dessert, Mr. Hayes?"

"She's right," Charlotte said to Anne. "How can she know the truth if you don't tell her?"

"Would you like some dessert, Mama?"

"You're still not going to say a word, are you?"

"Fine, Mama. If no one would like dessert, then Roy will make some coffee. I'm afraid I've got a terrible headache. I'm going upstairs to my room. I'm so sorry, Mr. Hayes. Perhaps another time you'll find us better behaved."

And Eve's aunt left the room like the Snow Queen exiting the stage, leaving Charlotte angrily staring at her plate, Emily in tears and Eve as white as the walls behind her, proudly displaying the endless generations of her family.

8

EVE SPENT SUNDAY regretting Saturday. The only bright spot in the whole disastrous evening had been Christopher's shrieks of delight when he'd torn the wrapping off his presents—especially the dinosaur.

So, okay, Mitch had a good handle on what four-year-olds liked. That did not negate the fact that they'd left as early as possible and she still felt as though she'd left a conversation unfinished. She wasn't sure with whom, though. Emily? Auntie Anne? Grandmother Best?

Grandmother was the worst of them all. Eve should never have brought Mitch along under false pretenses and gotten her hopes up. It wasn't as if she'd never been attracted to anyone before, and Grandmother knew it. She could hop on a MARTA train, for Pete's sake, and by the time she got downtown, she'd have seen any number of likely candidates for some fun between the sheets. So why did her family have to overreact like this?

Hmm. She might be able to work with that for the show. "Found Flings," they could call it. "Single on the Subway."

Never mind. Eve sighed and tried once again to focus on the script for Wednesday's show. When the phone rang, it was a relief.

"Hey." Mitch's smooth bass made her stomach do that shivery thing it did every time she heard his voice. "Just calling to make sure you were okay after last night."

"It really was as bad as I thought, wasn't it?" she asked, pushing aside the script and putting both elbows on the desk. "You're okay with me not inviting you in, right?"

"Sure. Not that I didn't want to come in, but I'm a big boy. Anyway, it was your typical family dinner, though more interesting than most. For what it's worth, I liked your family."

"Most of the time I do, too. I don't know what got into Grandmother. Usually she's the epitome of the Southern lady. I've never seen her scratch on poor Auntie Anne like that before. What was up with that whole thing about 'the truth'?"

"No idea. Probably some argument they got into before we arrived."

"And Emily watching the show," Eve said on a sigh. "Our demographics do include teenagers. It never occurred to me that Anne wouldn't approve."

"Are you sure it was the show she doesn't approve of?"

"What do you mean?"

"I got the feeling there was some jealousy floating around."

Jealous? Anne? Now, that was a stretch. "No. Couldn't be. I think she was just trying to head off any tendencies to celebrity worship in Emily, that's all.

Myself, I deplore that kind of thing—while I stack the tabloids in my grocery cart."

Mitch laughed. "Emily struck me as a sensible kid. What's a rainbow party?"

A chuckle bubbled in Eve's throat. "Go to UrbanDictionary.com and find out for yourself. And if you have any personal experience, I don't want to know about it."

"The only experience I'm interested in right now involves you. Any chance I can see you tonight?"

She glanced at the clock, then at the script. "I can't, Mitch. It's already half past eight and this script is close, but no cigar as yet."

"Tomorrow, then."

"Tomorrow. Though it won't be as much fun talking business in my office."

"I can think of plenty of fun things to do in your office."

"Don't you dare."

"What are you wearing?"

"My pajamas. Good night, Mitch."

He chuckled, and she realized he was teasing her. "Good night, honey pie."

Somehow, when he said it, it didn't come out at all the way Grandmother said it.

Talk about a verbal stroke in all the right places. Yum. She forced herself to hang up.

AS SHE DROVE IN to the station and got back into the swing of a Monday morning, Eve had to put aside personal thoughts of Mitch and of her family, and concentrate on the urgent issue at hand: the network—as represented by Mitch—coming back for a counteroffer.

Even if she didn't have the whole loyalty issue to deal with, the simple fact was that she couldn't leave her team behind and go national. Or if the unthinkable happened and she actually accepted CWB's proposal, she wanted to take them all with her. But how could she do that? Would they want her to move into a new affiliate facility? That might mean Cole's girls having to change schools or even cities. Jane and Perry might be looking at buying a house soon. What would the market be like somewhere else?

No, she couldn't go and that was that. *Just Between Us* succeeded because of her, but she only succeeded because of Nicole, Jane, Cole and Zach. One for all and all for one, that was going to be her motto if any more networks came sniffing around.

When she got back from an early afternoon appointment, Dylan Moore materialized in the door of her office before she'd even put her purse away.

"Are you sitting down?" he asked, even though he could see perfectly well she wasn't.

She pulled up her chair and sat. "I am now. Please don't tell me today's guest fell out."

"No, but Thursday's did."

"What?"

"Eve, that's not important. What is important is that the scout from SBN is in Dan Phillips's office even as we speak."

She stared at him, and he closed the door carefully behind his back.

"You told the CWB rep no, didn't you?"

"Repeatedly," Eve said. SBN? SBN was second only

to the biggies like ABC and FOX—and they were in
Dan's office? What the hell was Dan doing, entertain-
ing them without her there? What was going on?

"Keep an eye on them, Dylan," she said. "I'm sure
Dan will tell me all about it." He'd better. She'd pull
every word out of him with a pair of tweezers if he
didn't. "I'll be in makeup."

When she pushed open the door to the dressing
room, Zach and Jane looked up as if they were expecting to see…anyone but her.

As if she didn't show up ninety minutes before
airtime every week?

Zach pasted a grin on a face that had been far too
serious and got up. Jane stood, too.

"Hey, Eve," Zach said. "Don't mean to hold you up.
I was just on my way out."

"No problem." She looked from one to the other, but
Zach slipped behind her and out the door. She looked
at Jane, who pulled the makeup tray over and waved her
into the chair. "What was that all about?"

"Not much." Jane pulled Eve's hair back and
whipped the apron over her pintucked gauze blouse.
"We were only chatting."

"Why? Did they change the lighting or something?
Are we going with a different palette?"

"No, no. Personal stuff. Not to worry, he'll figure it
out."

To her knowledge, Zach wasn't in the habit of con-
fiding his "personal stuff" to Jane. The only thing they
had in common besides the show was the lottery. Eve
put two and two together with lightning speed.

"He's not thinking of quitting, too, is he?"

Eve closed her eyes as her friend began to dab on foundation. "He was talking out his options, that's all. You know Zach. He comes at things from every angle."

"But why would he come and talk to you? Did you tell him we talked on the weekend?"

"He wanted my opinion."

"I hope you told him it'd be crazy to quit now when there's no guarantee we'll ever see the lottery money."

"Not about that, and yes, I did tell him so. He wanted to know how you'd take it if he turned in his notice. I told him 'Not well,' but I think you know he has ambitions about filmmaking. It's only a matter of time, if you ask me."

"With eight million in the bank, you'd think a guy like him would be sailing off into the sunset with a bevy of blondes to swab his decks, not making indie films with no distribution."

"It's hard to know what Zach thinks. We're not *all* going to leave you, but it doesn't hurt to spare a thought for the future."

A cold finger of dread touched Eve's heart. Was that it? Was the fear of being left behind all that was triggering her anxiety?

She was no dummy. Back in Florida, Nana had made sure she'd talked with a grief counselor after the accident that had taken her parents. And she'd spent enough money on therapy since to know that she had a problem with that—being left behind. Deserted. Ditched as if she didn't matter.

Maybe that was why she was always the dumper in

her relationships, not the dumpee. She'd kept a weather eye open for signs that a man was losing interest, and she'd cut him off so fast that she left him blinking in the breeze of her departure. Rumor had it that Rafe Haddon was still showing up stag at charity dos. Maybe she'd scarred the poor guy for life. And what about Austin Taylor? And Sean Marshall? Should she give a little thought to an apology or at least an explanation there?

"Close your eyes," Jane murmured, and dabbed on eyelid foundation. "Relax."

"Do you think I should talk to Zach?" Eve asked her. "Or would he be upset that you told me?"

"Yes, and no, of course not. He knows we talk. That's why he came to me in the first place. Like I said, he was only testing his options, not typing up the letter, okay?"

Eve nodded—carefully—and Jane got down to business with eye shadow, liner and lipstick. Then Eve had half an hour to run over the script and ten minutes to warm up the guest, a female professor of human sexuality who looked old enough to play canasta with Charlotte. The prof's eyes held a sparkle, though, that told Eve they would both enjoy themselves in front of the cameras and the studio audience—and they did.

The audience loved it. Half the crowd flooded back to the station's lobby, where the prof was signing copies of her book, and Eve slipped into her office for a moment to decompress before she took the heavy makeup off.

Dylan poked his head in. "This a good time?"

"It depends on whether you're going to resign or not." She eyed the stack of pink telephone messages, each one bearing Dylan's spiky script.

"Not me. This is the most happening place in town. No, I wanted to report on my assignment."

Assignment? "Did you find a replacement for Thursday? Damn, I spent hours on that script."

"Not that one. You told me to keep an ear to the ground, remember? The scout from SBN?"

She'd completely forgotten. "What'd you find out? Is he gone?"

"She. And no. She took in the show and came back. I put her in the conference room to wait for you."

Eve stared at him. "I need to talk to Dan."

"He's in there with her, eating the doughnuts I brought for the crew this morning." He made a face. "Go on. You've got your game face on. Now's the perfect time."

Perfect for what? What was going on with Dan, anyway? Why was he running interference for her with SBN when he'd left her to CWB without a word?

Eve set her jaw. Lucky thing she'd worn red today. The power color. The color of sex and fame and confidence. She had a feeling she was going to need it.

MITCH HAD SPENT the rest of the weekend finding reasons to avoid calling Nelson Berg with an update. He'd fallen asleep to the sound of Eve's husky voice on the DVD recordings. Consequently, the sweet sound had whispered, as elusive and maddening as she was, in restless dreams where tanned skin and curves always seemed to be within touching distance, but never quite reachable.

Nelson, however, had made himself unavailable for most of Monday, so Mitch didn't feel guilty about not calling. First thing Tuesday, he called the station and asked for Dylan Moore.

"This is Mitchell Hayes from CWB," he said when he had Eve's assistant on the line.

"Nice to hear from you, Mr. Hayes," Dylan said. "Ms. Best told me you'd probably call, but she's in a meeting right now."

"That's okay. I don't want to interrupt her. I'd like to get on her calendar for lunch, if she's free."

"The show airs at three. She preps from eleven to noon, and then goes into makeup at one-thirty."

"Does she eat in between?"

"Not usually. Well, outside of a sandwich at her desk. She usually meets with the segment producers for a working lunch."

"If I brought her that sandwich, do you think she'd meet with me?"

Moore hesitated. "I honestly can't say, Mr. Hayes. The rep from SBN is here again and that's probably going to mess up everything she's got on her calendar."

Mitch dragged in a breath while he tried to process this unexpected punch to the gut. "SBN has a guy there already, huh?"

He'd known it would only be a matter of time. But two scouts on-site? Had someone sent out a press release announcing Eve and her show were up for grabs?

"Not a guy. A woman. Not that it matters, since I'm not supposed to disclose anything."

"It's Mackenzie Roussos, isn't it?" Mitch said flatly. "Tall, thin, dark hair, a smile like a shark closing in?"

"Yes."

Mitch sighed. Of all the luck. The TV business was a small world, and the New York nucleus even smaller. Everyone in production knew Mackenzie Roussos. Some people called her "Mac the Knife"—but never to her face.

What her presence meant to him, though, was that CWB was probably going to get left behind in the bidding war. Nelson's top offer for *Just Between Us* was the most generous the young network could afford. They'd been hoping they could get in and out with a contract before the big guns got wind of it, but that wasn't going to happen now. He could just imagine the kind of money Mackenzie Roussos was at this moment dangling in front of Eve. Which made it even more important that he see her.

"Mr. Moore, I need your help."

A pause. "My job is to assist Ms. Best, Mr. Hayes. And you can call me Dylan. Mr. Moore is my dad."

"You should call me Mitch, then. If Mackenzie Roussos is here, then it won't be long before all the vultures start landing and Eve's calendar is going to explode, along with her privacy and most of her free time. I can't do much, but if I get her away from there at least she'll have a little space."

"Which you'll then fill with a repeat of CWB's offer?" Dylan inquired with smooth politeness.

Mitchell's respect for the people Eve surrounded herself with went up a notch. "No, actually. I—we saw each other on the weekend. Socially. No business—or hardly any. She's under a lot of stress right now and I'd like to alleviate it some, if I can. As a friend. Not as Mackenzie Roussos's competitor."

Mitch could practically hear Dylan weighing the possibilities. "If you feed her, I can get her out of here."

He released a long breath. "Thanks, man. I appreciate it."

"There's a park on the other side of the apartment complex behind us. Be there with something for her at noon. And have her back by one-fifteen. No later."

Mitch gave him his cell phone number in case something went wrong, and rang off. He didn't have any ammunition up his sleeve to counter SBN's offer.

But he could certainly spike their guns with the help of a club sandwich.

So, at noon sharp, armed with two paper bags filled with the most appetizing lunch the deli at a nearby strip mall could provide, he stationed himself on a wrought-iron-and-cedar bench between two huge flowering bushes that gave him a good view up the street.

At five minutes past, he saw Eve Best striding down the sidewalk. She looked absolutely mouthwatering in a pair of skinny black jeans and a gauzy crimson top that tied with an oversize bow under her breasts. She also looked as though she could tear the bark off a tree with her teeth.

She hadn't seen him yet. Pausing in the middle of the sidewalk near the rock wall that formed the park's boundary, she fisted both hands on her hips and scanned the area. He stood up and waved.

Her mouth opened in a soundless O and it suddenly occurred to him that he didn't know what kind of story Dylan Moore had told her to get her down here.

Obviously, it hadn't been the truth.

Unexpectedly, she laughed, and the anger went out of her body. "Well, you're a big improvement on the person I was expecting," she said. "What are you doing here?"

"I'm your lunch date." He held up a hand, palm out. "Scout's honor. Dylan and I set you up."

"You sure did." She swung a leg over the stone wall and joined him. "He told me one of Jane's ex-boyfriends was down here, wanting me to help get them back together."

"And you believed him?" He handed her a sandwich and a tall paper cup filled with a lime-and-kiwi smoothie. The counter guy had insisted that Eve Best came in there all the time, and that was her favorite. With a grimace, Mitch had bought it and ordered a tall bottle of water for himself. He was discovering that if you spent more than fifteen minutes outside in the Atlanta heat, you'd need it.

"Sure I believed him. Despite the fact that she's crazy about Perry, an ex of Jane's has been surprisingly persistent since the news broke about the lottery." She bit into the sandwich as though it was someone's neck. "And before this I've never had a reason not to trust anything Dylan told me."

"It wasn't his fault. We conspired to get you out of there for a break."

"I'm glad you did. My calendar probably won't be, but I'll let Dylan take care of that."

"Smoothie okay?"

She took a sip and nodded. "Dylan told you to go to Scarlett's, didn't he?"

"No. I wound up there on my own. But the counter guy said you liked those."

She sighed and put her drink on the ground. "That was nice of you. This whole idea is nice. I have to admit I'm not having the best day."

Mitch smothered his smile in a bite of his pastrami sandwich. "No problem. I know from experience that Mac the Knife can be a handful."

A smile flickered at the corners of her mouth. "Word travels fast. Is that what the people in New York call her?"

"Not to her face. It's Ms. Roussos then. I'm betting she pitched you an offer you couldn't refuse."

Eve began to relax against the wood slats of the bench back. A cluster of pink flowers from the bush nodded over her shoulder.

What was it about her that seemed to attract flowers? Her roses seemed to press against her door. Strange bushes cuddled up to her in the middle of the day. What next? An adoring dandelion wrapped around her ankle?

He resisted the urge to check.

No, he was probably just projecting his own desires onto innocent plants. It wouldn't take much for him to press up against her door, begging for entry, or to nuzzle the bit of shoulder left bare by her sleeveless top. Or even, if it came to that, to press a kiss on the inside of that delectable ankle.

In fact, he'd love to press any number of kisses on any skin he could—

"Yep," she said in answer to his question. "And surprise, surprise, my boss thinks I should take it."

He blinked and focused abruptly. What left field had that come out of? "Take it? Isn't he the one who benefits most if you stay?"

"Not if our happy little independent becomes an SBN affiliate." She bit into her sandwich again. "Which—gee, how did I not know this?—has been his ambition for years. He has big plans for his production company, apparently."

"Don't tell me." Mitch toasted her with his water bottle. "Part of the reason he gave you his support despite all odds was because he knew he was on to a good thing? A show that could get him the attention he wanted from the networks?"

"Bingo." A sip of the green smoothie and another bite. "You're a lot quicker off the draw than I was. It took me a good half hour to get it. And then when I did, there was your friend Mackenzie Roussos standing there with a fistful of dollars, waving them in my face like they were supposed to get my attention." She snorted. "I just won the lottery, for God's sake. Money is not going to get my attention right now. A really good financial planner, maybe. Not money. I should have known something was up the minute I heard she was meeting with him before she talked to me."

"I'm glad I didn't meet with him first, then. Or I'd have been suspect."

She shot him a glance, and he saw the sunlight flicker on her smooth skin, lighting tiny spangles of auburn in her hair. Did she have any idea that she looked like an elemental goddess, made of crimson and fire, wrapped around with flowers?

Probably not. And he'd better stop thinking about throwing himself on that fire and breathing in the scent of crushed flowers, if he knew what was good for him.

"Suspect?" she repeated. "No. In fact…" Her voice trailed away. "It's weird. I have no idea why I'm blabbing all this about your competitor. There must be some sort of unfair competition law I'm breaking."

"I doubt it. But how many people do you know who would understand? Dan Phillips? Your friends?"

"They would sympathize, but there's a lot to grasp here. The risks. The consequences."

"Especially when some of them are going to be affected by the results, no matter what your decision is."

Eve nodded. "I've been chasing that in my head, and I'm no closer to a decision than I was when you left my office on Friday."

"How can that be? You said no."

"I did. And then I started to think. What if I said yes? What would change? Can I keep my team? What would be best for everyone?"

"Why don't you call a meeting and ask them?"

She looked at him with a wry expression. "At the rate we're going, they'll all have resigned before I can schedule it. It's this damned lottery." She waved a hand, as if Atlanta were somehow responsible. "We haven't seen the money, and we won't until this lawsuit is settled. Despite that, everyone wants to quit and make huge life changes on the prospect of it alone. I feel like that kid with his finger in the dam. Every time I convince someone to hang in there and stay, I hear someone else is reconsidering the options."

"That's got to be tough. It's hard to make a decision that will benefit everyone if they leave. It becomes moot."

"See, there's your strategy." Another bite of the sandwich. "You can talk my team into resigning, and then you'll only have me to convince to come to the network. Not that you'll have any vestige of a show once that happens, of course."

He watched her finish her sandwich, crumple the wrapper and toss it back in the bag. "You really care about these people, don't you? You want to make the right decision for them, not yourself."

She stretched out her legs and crossed her ankles, holding her smoothie loosely in her lap. "Nothing wrong with that. Without them, I wouldn't be here talking to you. We wouldn't have the show that we do."

"What does SBN propose?"

"Oh, they have all kinds of proposals. But the one Ms. Roussos and Dan spent the most time on was the one where I pack up and move to New York." She paused. "Like that's going to happen."

"New York? You mean, even if Dan got his wish and merged into the network, he wouldn't get to keep you? Isn't that counterproductive, from his point of view?"

"Maybe. Or maybe he's dazzled at being invited to swim in the big boys' pond. But if he gets the affiliation, he can attract some big names. Maybe even a news anchor or two. Big advertising, lots of resources. He wouldn't need the revenue *Just Between Us* brings in. Everybody wins."

"Except you. And the team."

"Cole Crawford would probably lose his job," she agreed. "But Zach and Jane and Nicole wouldn't. Every show needs good freelance production people, and they're already in place."

"They could go to New York with you, in that case."

"I don't think so. They have people they love, and their plans might not include a big move like that. And that's as it should be."

"And what about you?" he asked. "How would you like New York?"

"I'd hate it," she said flatly.

That pretty much answered that. The bright, fragile hope he'd had burned out.

9

ON WEDNESDAY, Mackenzie Roussos arrived for her seven-thirty meeting with Eve in a towering temper, brought on by the fact that a scout from CBS was waiting in the lobby for his eight o'clock.

"I thought we were scheduled to chat for an hour," she said, her mouth stretching in a smile that Eve could tell was an effort for her.

"We were, and I'm sorry," Eve told her. "My assistant is doing the best he can to accommodate everyone."

"It feels like six-thirty New York time," the other woman said.

"I'm glad there's fresh coffee in the kitchen for you, then."

And Mac the Knife was forced to be satisfied with only twenty-five minutes in which to try to convince Eve to go along with what both the network and Dan Phillips wanted.

The rep from CBS, at least, had a sense of humor and a nice delivery of the same proposal. He'd already met with Dan for dinner the night before.

There seemed to be a pattern developing here, and Eve didn't like it much. In fact, the more network people who turned up in the lobby, the more she wanted to collar Mitchell Hayes and run away to the country with him. They could find a pretty inn and spend a week straight doing something about her lack of focus—or rather, her inability to focus on much else besides his mouth and his hands—and what he might be able to do with both.

When Dylan again suggested that a walk in the park might clear her head, she fled the station gratefully, and the sight of Mitch relaxing on the bench was like a glass of cold lemonade on a hot day.

"Hey, beautiful," he greeted her, and slid over to make room. She toed off her sandals and, with a sigh, let her feet rest in the cool grass.

He handed her a wrapped sandwich and a smoothie. "Your guy at Scarlett's says the watermelon is an experiment. If you like it, he's going to call it 'Eve-ning in Paradise.'"

Eve groaned at the pun and took a sip. "Hey, this is good. It ain't lime, but it's good." She glanced at him. "Is there a bug on my feet? Why are you looking at them?"

He settled back on the bench and unwrapped his sandwich. "I have this theory about you and plant life."

Turkey and cranberry with cream cheese spread. Eve sighed with satisfaction. "I think you need to get out more."

He ignored her. "You just look good in the great outdoors. As if you belong there. Plants seem to like you."

"I don't have my Nana's green thumb—you should have seen our place in Florida—but I'm most comfortable in the garden. It relaxes me. Plus I can see direct results of what I do. Sometimes in television that's hard to estimate."

"Nielsen ratings not good enough for you?"

"We don't get those. We're an independent. Fan mail is a better indicator anyway. Some of it's good, some bad. By the way, both SBN and CBS are here now."

"I knew it was only a matter of time. I'd keep a close watch on your boss, Dan Phillips. Those scouts are players, and they represent serious money. It's going to be hard for him to stay out of the decision-making process. Harder still for him to resist putting pressure on you."

"He knows how I feel. Besides, my career and where I go aren't his decision, no matter what he thinks." She savored the tart flavor of cranberry on her tongue and mentally waved the thought of Dan away. "I don't want to talk about work anymore. Tell me about your life in New York."

He exhaled sharply in place of a chuckle. "What life? I jet around the country scouting shows. The baristas in the Starbucks at JFK have more interesting stories to tell."

"So are you happy doing what you do?"

He met her gaze and shrugged. "I get my joy in other ways, like Music on the Street. And lately, seeing you."

"Charmer."

"I meant it, Eve. I'm developing this amazing capacity for fooling myself. I have an ultimatum from my boss about getting your signature by close of business today, and I don't even care. In fact, I've convinced my conscience that seeing you has nothing to do with work. That it's a pleasure I savor every day with no ethical relation to the whole reason I'm here."

There was none of his usual teasing in his eyes. In fact, his gaze on her was intense to the point of sheer eroticism. Words failed her, and she licked her lips.

"You make it sound like a bad thing."

"It isn't. And just so you know, there's no one waiting at home. Like you, the care and feeding of a relationship is too much for me under normal circumstances. But I'm beginning to wonder exactly what 'normal' is. And whether I want to tolerate it anymore."

What was he saying? Was he leading up to something? And more important, how did she feel about it?

It was one thing to have a few sexy interludes with an attractive man. To banter and touch, to enjoy the longing and hint at something more. Like a game—one that kept the attraction simmering on the surface because it helped to balance the stresses of a decision that was creeping up on her faster than she wanted. But what if he made her dip below the surface? To start something bigger?

Could she handle that? Did she want more than— let's face it—a hot fling with a man who would fly out of her life in a few days?

Or was that even what he was talking about? Eve's everyday honesty faltered—and that in itself should tell her something.

She had to think about this properly. Somewhere where he wasn't sitting within touching distance, looking scrumptious and casual in an off-duty linen shirt and khakis.

A glance at her watch told her she was saved. She

crumpled her paper and drained her smoothie. "Let's put a bookmark there and talk more about this later, okay? I have to get back."

"Sure." He looked easy and relaxed, but if it had been her waiting for an answer and getting none, Eve wasn't sure she'd handle it so well. Especially if she had the ultimatum he did. "Give me a call."

Back at the station, Nicole slipped into Eve's office with a doomsday look on her face. Once again, Eve put her wayward thoughts in their compartment in her brain and smiled in a way she hoped was encouraging. "What's up, girlfriend?"

"I finally managed to get Dr. Birdsall to commit to Friday." Nicole sounded out of breath, as if she'd run down the hall as soon as she'd hung up the phone. "But we can't do Friday because that's the town-hall show. And we still have a hole for tomorrow. Cole needs to run a teaser during the six o'clock news and I don't know what to do."

Eve thought for a few seconds. "How about this? We'll switch and have the town-hall show tomorrow, so run the usual teaser tonight. Instead of having the audience react to her talking about how men and women hide their motivations when they deal with the opposite sex, why don't we tape segments of people telling their stories, and Dr. Birdsall can analyze what's really going on when she comes on Friday."

"Brilliant," Nicole breathed.

"Bill it as a two-parter, a before-and-after, whatever you want. We're good at making something out of nothing. You can handle it."

"Thanks, Eve." She vanished into her office, leaving Eve with her thoughts until she had to go into makeup.

Part of her admitted that it was crazy to talk to Mitch the way she did during these stolen hours. He was on the same side as the dark forces, i.e. the networks. But on the other hand, she was sure she'd go around the bend without his calm views on what amounted to a crisis situation.

Who else understood what she was going through? Who else seemed to know exactly what it took to change her perspective or set her heart at ease when her mind was blasting away at a hundred miles an hour?

She knew it was foolish and couldn't last, but she put Mitch the Scout into a compartment labeled Business and put Mitch the Sexy Confidant into one labeled Friend. Okay, so it had a little subheading called Possible Lover in very tiny font below that. But anyway, there she'd keep the two of them until she was forced to combine them.

In the meantime, she was going to take his advice. The script that had been so troublesome on the weekend went off better than she expected. When she got back from taping, she sent out a scheduler message to the computers and PDAs of all her staff. She had just enough time to work up a business case before everyone gathered in the conference room for what they thought was the production meeting. She was going to tack another item onto the agenda and find out once and for all if her team was going to melt away on her, or stay just that—a team.

IF JENNA HAMILTON had been ten years younger, she'd have been running after Dylan Moore before he knew what was up. But since Kevin Wade had been haunting her dreams for the last couple of weeks, she was content to give Dylan an appreciative smile as he ushered her out of the lobby and past the studios.

"Everyone named in the suit is in the conference room already," he told her. "Eve asked me to convey her appreciation for fitting the meeting into your schedule."

"No problem," she murmured. "You'd be surprised how much the case is on my mind anyway."

When she entered the room, Eve stood to greet her. "Jenna, I'm so glad you could come. You remember everyone, right?"

In a single sweep, Jenna catalogued the people whose names had become as familiar to her as her own. Cole Crawford, the producer who'd been with *Just Between Us* since its inception. Twenty-four-year-old Zach Haas, the camera operator. California girl and story segment producer Nicole Reavis, whom she'd already met, and Jane Kurtz, who did makeup—maybe not the flashiest job, but Jenna had a feeling that Eve Best depended on her for a lot more than that.

Cole tilted his chair back and crossed his arms comfortably over his chest as Jenna sat opposite him in an empty chair. "Gee, boss, I wonder what this could be about?"

Eve gave him a winning smile. "Very funny. You've seen the reps from three networks around here. You've seen the show's ratings, not to mention the press we're getting. I figured we could use a powwow to catch everyone up and strategize a bit."

"And for this we need a lawyer?" Nicole glanced at Jenna. "Not that I'm not glad to see you, Jenna."

Jenna smiled at her. "Thanks. As CATL-TV's corporate counsel, I'm only here to give y'all information and advice if you need it. We're all playing on the same team, so your concerns are my concerns."

"So, let me tell you what I know, and then you can tell me—" Eve paused "—whatever you know. Or want to know. Or anything else you have on your minds." She glanced around the table. "Let's talk about the networks first. As you know, Mitchell Hayes from CWB came to see me last Friday. We've met a couple of times since then."

"Does that mean they're the front runners?" Jane asked. "You haven't met more than once with the others, right?"

A flush that wasn't the result of Jane's makeup tinged Eve's cheeks. What was that about? Jenna wondered.

"Only because they haven't been in Atlanta as long. Mackenzie Roussos from SBN got here Monday, and then Chad Everard from CBS showed up this morning. I've heard what they have to say and had Dan's input, as well." She passed out a sheet of paper with four columns of bullet points. "What I don't have is your input, and no decision gets made around here without it."

Jenna took her sheet. It listed all three networks' proposed deal points, boiled down to their essence, as well as groupings of pros and cons. "Very nice."

Eve shrugged. "We can't talk about the future unless we all have the facts. So. I'll go straight to the bottom

line. We have three options. One, we say no to everybody and stay in Atlanta at CATL-TV as we have been.
We enjoy what we've achieved and build on it. Two, we
accept the offer of either SBN or CBS, and pack up and
go to New York."

Zach, Jenna noted, lifted his head like a puppy
scenting the great outdoors. Jane frowned, Cole's arms
crossed more tightly, and Nicole looked mildly interested. Hmm.

"Or three," Eve went on, "we accept CWB's offer,
which is substantially lower than SBN's, and stay here
as one of their affiliates. They're a young network, still
growing, so they don't have the advertising weight the
bigger ones do. But we will have national coverage in
the small and medium-sized markets, though it'll take
a while to penetrate the big ones."

Jenna broke the silence as six people considered the
sheet of paper. "In case any of you are factoring the
lottery win into this—which I'm sure you are—" She
hesitated for a second. "Don't. Ms. Skinner has
informed me through her attorney that she's not
prepared to settle for anything less than an equal share
of the prize money. That means we will be taking the
case to court. Please consider the networks' offers in-
dependently of any funds you might or might not
receive from Lot'O'Bucks."

Zach groaned, and Cole uncrossed both arms with
such force he smacked the arms of his chair. Nicole
jumped, and Eve frowned.

"You guys, we knew this," Eve said. "I've told a
couple of you that counting on the lottery money when

it's been challenged is like counting on it to snow on the Fourth of July. We'd be stupid to put our lives out on a limb—not to mention our finances and futures—for something that may never happen. That's why we need to move forward together on this. I want to know how you feel about the networks' proposals."

"I'm for New York," Zach said immediately.

"I'm not," Cole threw out with the force of an air gun. "I'm not uprooting my girls and dragging them off to a place that may as well be another planet."

"Yeah, but think of the career opportunities," Zach said. "You could give them the kind of life they'd never get here."

"What, away from their family and friends? And what am I supposed to do with them while I'm working the hours that we do? Nuh-uh." Cole's arms crossed again, and this time they weren't relaxed and comfortable. "No networks for me. I'll stay here and produce a different show, if I have to."

"Jane?" Eve looked at the end of the table. "What's your opinion?"

"I'd have to think about it for more than five minutes, but my instinct is to go with CWB and stay put. Yeah, the coverage isn't as great, but we've worked up to regional success. We can work up to the big-city markets, too." Jane glanced at Nicole, who sat on her left. "What do you think, Nic? You're the one with out-of-state experience."

Nicole looked uncomfortable at being the center of everyone's attention. Or maybe, Jenna speculated, being the new kid on the block, she didn't think her opinion would hold as much weight as that of the others.

"I—I'm conflicted," she admitted. "Devon's family and background are all here. Mine is on the West Coast. A move to New York would take him away from everything he knows, and me even farther away from what I know. I'd talk it over with him before I gave a decision, of course, but if we're looking for gut reactions, I'd say no to the big networks. Let us stay as we are, where we're happy doing what we do, or let us go with CWB. Either way, we get to stay in Atlanta."

Jenna let everyone absorb this for a moment, and then said, "And what about you, Eve? This decision is going to impact you the most. You're the one bearing the biggest weight, here."

"Are you hinting that I need to go back to the South Beach Diet?" Eve cracked.

Jenna grinned at her. "Not a chance, girl. Those curves are bringin' in the male demographic in a big way."

Eve's smile dimmed, but didn't disappear altogether. "I have to say I'm with Jane. The CWB offer has a lot going for it. We've built our success in a regional market, and they specialize in that. So what if the big guys have the big markets sewn up—or think they do? We can work up to it. Give 'em a run for their money." She looked around at everyone, and Jenna saw her straighten her shoulders. "I think we're ready for the big time, guys. I know I am. We have a good show, a terrific team and a lot to bring to folks outside of Atlanta. I think going with CWB is smart. Not so ambitious we fall on our faces, but still a reach outside of our comfort zone. It'll stretch us. Make us better, different. We don't give up anything, and we get a lot. What do you say?"

Jane put up her hand. "CWB."

So did Cole. "I agree."

Nicole said, "Me, too."

"That's four. Zach?" Eve prompted.

Zach, Jenna thought, had the kind of face that would usually get him what he wanted. But this was bigger than he was. What kind of response would he give?

Zach sighed. "Well, I can't very well go to New York by myself. Not after everything that happened there. So if you guys are determined to stay, then I'll stay here, too."

"Woohoo!" Jane leaped up and gave him a hug, and suddenly it was as if their team had won the hometown game. Everyone hugged the person next to them, and Eve practically disappeared in Cole Crawford's big embrace.

Only Jenna stood apart, feeling for the first time that tug of absence deep inside. That urge to be a part of something bigger than just family and the horde of girl-friends she went clubbing with on Saturday nights.

When Cole turned toward her and gave her a big kiss, as if she'd had some part in this decision they'd made all on their own, she finally identified the feeling.

She wanted someone of her own to celebrate with. To be a part of. To build something with.

And she wanted that someone to be Kevin Wade.

10

MITCH ALMOST MISSED the call when his cell phone jingled at quarter past six Wednesday afternoon. He backed out of the hotel room's shower, turned off the water and sprinted over to the bed. The phone vibrated against the glossy veneer of the nightstand.

"Mitchell Hayes."

"Mitch, it's Eve."

It wasn't his fault he couldn't control the silly grin that spread over his face at the sound of that husky, musical voice. Good thing there was no one here to see what a goofball he was. He sank onto the coverlet. "Hey, Eve."

"What could I tell you that would make you really happy right now?"

He paused for a moment to consider several dazzling possibilities. "You're standing outside my door wrapped in a velvet ribbon and nothing else?"

"You're lucky I don't have speakerphone on," she chided. "Try again."

"You're calling to ask me out?"

"Maybe. But before that."

Maybe? "Before, after, I don't care. The answer is yes, I'd love to go out. When should I pick you up?"

"Would you listen?" Her voice trembled with laughter. "I'm talking business, here."

"You said what would make *me* happy, not the network. Okay, what happened between now and one-fifteen, when we said goodbye in the park?"

"I met with my team and presented our options to them. I told them we could make no changes…stay in Atlanta and go with CWB…or move to New York and go with one of the big networks."

"And which did they choose?" He dragged his mind off where he might take her tonight—besides his hotel room, that is. He was really in fine shape when seeing her had become more important than the outcome of the deal. And speaking of that, he'd been inches away from packing it in and going back to headquarters to take his lumps. With the arrival of Mackenzie Roussos and Chad Everard and their bottomless pockets, he'd figured CWB wouldn't have a chance at succeeding.

Money always won. Always.

"They want to stay in Atlanta and become a CWB affiliate," she told him, triumph in her tone. "It may not get us as big a reach as SBN or CBS, but all of us know that reaching sometimes means overreaching, and that just makes you fall on your face. The 'enthusiastically conservative' approach to business has served us well so far. We figure we should just keep doing it that way."

"I'm…delighted," he managed from under his amazement. They'd chosen CWB. He'd won. After two failed deals in his immediate history, he didn't have to go back to New York and face Nelson Berg's derision. He was going to be able to keep his job—and meet the man's damn deadline to boot. It was a miracle. "Amazed. Happy. Thank you."

"There's one caveat, though," she said. "I want a guarantee that I can keep my team together. They've all agreed in principle to coming on board, and I realize we'll have to negotiate compensation and all that. But what I don't want is for the network to lay them off as soon as we sign the contract, and plug its own people in."

"Fair enough," he allowed, trying to breathe through the tight feeling in his chest. That feeling that meant he was holding back a shout of triumph. "I'll present that as part of the deal."

"I think the fact that we got an agreement at all calls for a celebration," she said, "and I'm not talking about a walk in the park, either."

"I can take your whole team to dinner. We'll max out the network credit card in a show of good faith."

"I hope you will, but not tonight. Tonight I want it to be just you and me. You've helped me so much this week. I wish there were some way to thank you."

"You already found it," he said fervently. "But sure. I'd love that. I usually spend the evenings watching the competition and thinking about you anyway."

This time she laughed. "You know, you really should find a more romantic way to phrase these things."

He had to smile, too. "Ah, but if I think about you and romance together, I get into trouble. Look what happened the last time, at your uncle's. And at the Ashmere mansion."

In his mind's eye, for the thousandth time, he saw her silhouetted against that ivy-covered wall, her skin pale in the moonlight, her gown hugging the curves he still hungered to touch and taste. And then later, in the car, when she—

His body throbbed at the thought.

She had no idea how difficult it was to see her every day in the park and not beg her to come back to the hotel with him. To sit next to her on the bench and talk about the television business, when all he wanted to do was to lay her down in the grass. To explore the splendid curves revealed by her beaded, sometimes plunging necklines while with each inch of discovery, the chemistry all but ignited between them.

"I remember every second of what happened at the Ashmere mansion." Her tone dropped to almost a whisper.

"Is your office door closed?" His own voice dropped, too, though there was no one within four walls of him.

"Yes."

"I remember how silky your skin is. How sexy your mouth is when you talk. When I'm not with you, I fantasize about you. Basically, I'm hooked on you twenty-four seven."

"You fantasize about me?" Her whisper had become downright breathless.

"Oh, yeah. In my mind, we've been on your desk, on my desk, at my hotel, in the park, on carpets of those pink flowers, you name it. We have an amazing love life for two people who have never seen each other naked."

She giggled. "You've seen me nearly naked."

His body stiffened with appreciation. "One of my fondest memories. I could write entire sonnets to that moment, I swear. Have I told you how much I like that red gauze top you had on yesterday? That was good for a real dream about you last night, not just your standard daytime fantasy."

"I was wearing a bra, you bad boy," she whispered.

"Mmm," he rumbled. "A push-up. And a fine example of its kind. I and a couple of million male viewers thank you."

"It didn't show anything!" she squeaked. "I had the director and the guys in the control booth double-check. Both backlighting *and* spots."

"I bet they enjoyed that. No, you only showed enough to run my concentration right off the rails. It was more the total effect. The jeans were great, too. Have I told you what a pretty rear view you have?"

"No, poor thing. With you, it gets no attention."

"I am pretty consistent," he admitted. "I hope you know what this conversation is doing to me, even as we speak."

"If it's anything like what it's doing to me, it's going to be difficult to get out of here without someone suspecting I have a very hot date."

"You do. How soon can I pick you up?"

"Um, as soon as the swelling goes down?"

"Well, yes, that's a given. Say, seven-thirty? That gives you seventy-five minutes."

"We're going to dinner, right?" she asked. "Just checking."

"Dinner," he promised. "And now that negotiations

are over, after the champagne, I really, really, want you for dessert."

It took ten minutes of steady concentration before Mitch could turn off the sensual images blending into one another in his head, and reduce his hard-on to manageable proportions. He had to call Nelson and tell him the good news, and he simply couldn't do that when Eve filled his mind and affected his body in such an unbusinesslike fashion.

All he wanted to do was think about her and what was to come this evening. And he would—after he called in to report.

Mitch walked back into the bathroom and took his shower, with the water a little cooler than usual. Once he was shaved and dressed, he picked up his cell and hit Autodial.

Nelson Berg answered on the first ring.

"It's Mitch."

"Just how long do you plan to spend down there enjoying Southern hospitality?" Nelson barked. "You got some kind of Scarlett O'Hara complex says you'll think about doing the deal tomorrow, or what? Let me tell you, tomorrow never—"

"The deal's done, Nelson."

That stopped him. For all of two seconds.

"When did this happen?"

"Just now. Consider your deadline met. It's done for all intents and purposes, anyway. Eve Best called me to say she'd reached an agreement in principle with her staff, and then I called you."

"Did she, now? How about that."

Mitch's forehead creased. "You sound surprised. Didn't you think I could pull it off?"

"Oh, I knew you'd give it everything you had. It was that or the job postings on Craigslist."

"Your confidence humbles me, Nelson."

"It keeps you young bucks on your toes. So how soon will they be coming over? I've got a lot of logistics to handle once the process starts."

"We have to iron that out, but I can't see it going longer than six months. We may not make the November sweeps, but we'll definitely get May."

"I want November," Nelson said immediately. "Get 'em on board by September at the latest."

"I'll do my best."

"Damn right you will. You might have pulled off this one, but anybody can do a handoff. I can replace you."

Deep in Mitch's gut, anger began to bubble. "Nelson, anybody ever send you to management training? Because the reward-and-punishment method of motivation is really getting old."

"I don't need to punish people who do their jobs properly," Nelson snapped. "And if you don't like it, you don't have to stick around."

"Fine. I can quit, if you want. Before we get Eve Best's signature on this contract. Mackenzie Roussos and Chad Everard are both here. I'm sure they'd be happy to step in with theirs."

Nelson swore so colorfully that Mitch wondered if he'd been in the navy at some point. Back in the dark ages. Before managers learned to lead by example instead of by threatening everyone in sight.

But Nelson also appreciated a man who had a spine. Mitch might not be a shark like Roussos, or a glamour boy like Everard, but he could bring in the results with the best of them.

Nelson ran out of steam eventually and surprised Mitch with a change of subject. "So, how'd you pull it off? Did you take my advice and romance her? That always works with women."

As if Nelson would know. The guy had been divorced, what, three times?

"I did not. She needed someone to talk to and I stood in as a sounding board."

"Talk to?" From his tone, you'd think Eve had demanded that Mitch eat raw squid.

"There aren't a lot of women in this region in her position, Nelson. And it's not like she can call up Oprah or Ellen DeGeneres for a pep talk. I've been around this industry a while and seen a lot of shows in production. She appreciates a high-level view."

"As long as you're not exchanging industry secrets," Nelson warned. "You know my opinions about that."

"If we're going to be on the same payroll they won't be secrets," he pointed out. "I plan to bring her on board with CWB's culture, org structure, all that. In time. Not now."

"Too soon for that," Nelson agreed. "Get her John Hancock on that contract and she'll be inundated with all that stuff. Good work, Hayes. When are you coming back?"

"When I get the aforesaid John Hancock," Mitch replied drily. "And we have a few things to iron out. For instance, she wants assurance that her team will stay together under our management."

"Why? You've seen one producer, you've seen them all."

"It's not just the producer. It's the cameraman, the main story coordinator, the makeup artist who happens to be her best friend."

Nelson made a noise that expressed his opinion of that. "I sent you down there to get Eve Best. I don't care about her friend the makeup artist. Those people are a dime a dozen."

"In my opinion, it would be a mistake to upset the status quo," Mitch warned. "This team has created a winner. Making the change from independent to network is going to be disruptive enough. I'd recommend strongly that we not make any further changes."

"I'll think about it," Nelson conceded grudgingly. "We can always give them short contracts and unload them in a year. I'll talk it over with the honchos in our teleconference on Monday."

Mitch acknowledged this was the best he could expect for now. He and Nelson both knew that Eve had them over a barrel. If they didn't meet her conditions, she could pull out and remain as she was, no harm done. At worst, she could call SBN or CBS and play hardball with them, cutting CWB out of the running altogether.

"So, what else?" Nelson asked.

"Tonight we're going to—" he stopped.

"What?"

"Review the list of upcoming guest segments," he lied. "That's it for now. Talk to you later, Nelson."

His boss rang off with his customary abruptness and Mitch snapped his cell phone shut.

He needed to watch his mouth. Because there was no way he was telling anyone that he and Eve were meeting for dinner. Or about what they had planned after that.

EVE PUT THE RECEIVER down quietly and marveled at what Mitch Hayes could do to her with words alone. Oh, and the low, sexy voice didn't hurt, either. That was the second time she'd skated close to having phone sex with the man—and her blood was hot, and her body softened and ready. If Mitch had been here, she'd have locked the door and jumped him.

As it was, she had to get a grip on her rioting responses. Her first duty was to let Dan know the team's decision before he heard the news in the hall.

For a few moments, she concentrated on slowing her heartbeat and calming her breathing.

Come on, seven-thirty. This would be the shortest meeting on record.

She climbed the stairs to the station's third floor and tapped on Dan Phillips's door. When she heard him call, "Come in," she pushed it open.

And stopped on the threshold. "Oh, sorry. I didn't know you were with someone."

Mackenzie Roussos uncurled her lanky frame, which topped Eve's by about four inches, from the squashy chair in the corner. "Nice to see you, Eve," she said. "Great show today. I'm looking forward to sticking around for the town-hall show tomorrow, too."

"Thanks," she replied, watching Mac the Knife the way a bird would watch an approaching cat. Shrugging off the last lingering thought of Mitch, her senses went on alert. "We never know what to expect with those. I think that's why they get the highest ratings during the week. There's something mesmerizing about unpredictability."

"There's something mesmerizing about *Just Between Us,* period," Mackenzie purred. "I really think it would be a fabulous fit for SBN."

Well, there was a perfect opening for you. "Actually, that's what I came to discuss with Dan." She glanced at him, then back at the other woman, and smiled. Let her make what she wanted of *that.* "In confidence. Do you mind, Mackenzie?"

Roussos smiled and snagged her silk jacket off the coat tree and her Dooney & Bourke briefcase from the floor. "Not a bit. I love it when you talk about me and my network behind my back. Later, Dan."

She closed the door behind her, and Eve sank into the other chair, which was a hard-backed one close to the chaotic pile that concealed his desk. What had they been talking about? Was she making him pie-in-the-sky promises about the future of his production company if he guaranteed that SBN would get the show? Or was she here for more personal reasons? Just how much influence did a high-flying woman like Mackenzie Roussos have over a middle-aged, independent station owner who hankered for a taste of the big time?

There was no way to ask these questions, and she had a job to do. For a moment, she wondered how to begin, but he saved her that decision.

"Production meeting go okay?"

She nodded. "Town-hall prep is pretty straightforward. Give the audience a topic and stand out of the way of flying objects." He chuckled, and she went on, "I was glad to have some extra time to talk over the networks' offers with everyone at once."

Dan eyed her, giving away nothing. "And?"

"I gave them the three options, and we talked over the ramifications of each one. In the end, it was nearly unanimous."

Another pause. Then Dan said, "You want me to read it in tomorrow's paper, or what?"

Ouch. She'd thought he'd be mellower after being schmoozed for however long Mackenzie had been closeted in here with him. Eve took a deep breath. "Everyone wants to go with CWB."

His face froze.

She rushed on, "All of us except maybe Zach have reasons for wanting to stay in Atlanta. Me included. I'm just getting to know my extended family after being away for so long. Cole doesn't want to uproot his kids. Nicole would rather not go even farther east and—"

"CWB?" he asked, as if she hadn't even been talking. "You chose that Podunk network over SBN and CBS?"

"Yes."

"Are you completely insane?" He pushed his chair back and stalked around it. For a second Eve wondered if he had a predisposition to violence she didn't know about, and then he passed her and began to walk a tight circle on the area rug. "Their offer wasn't even half as generous as SBN's. What are you people *thinking?*"

"We're thinking about our lives," she said carefully, watching him. "About the quality of them. And frankly, with the exception of Jenna Hamilton, nobody in that room really cares about SBN's money right now. We have enough of our own."

"You would have if Liza Skinner hadn't shown up, dragging her sour grapes into this. You can't depend on that money, Eve. By the time she gets through with you, most of it will have gone on legal fees, and twenty years from now you'll get a check for a thousand bucks."

"Maybe." Eve tried to keep her voice steady. Mitch had warned her, hadn't he? She should have listened to him—and been ready. She should have realized how invested Dan was in going with one of the big networks. She should have seen the significance of all these tête-à-têtes with Mackenzie Roussos. "But even leaving the money out of it, CWB still has the best deal. No one wants to go to New York. Period."

"Maybe I do," he ground out.

"Then go, if you want to. Sell the station outright to CWB instead of becoming an affiliate. Or sell Driver Productions to SBN and syndicate the heck out of it."

He glared at her, and she realized that disappointment in her decision had clouded his ability to see reason at the moment. She valued her relationship with Dan, and staying any longer meant they'd probably both say things they'd regret.

"Look, I'm sorry that this is disappointing for you. But you'll see in the long run that it's best for the team. And that's what we all want, right?"

He threw himself into the squashy chair—which was probably still warm from Mackenzie's shapely behind—and stared out the window.

"Maybe we can talk about it later," she offered, and slipped out, closing the door behind her.

Thank God she had Mitch to look forward to, she thought, as she clattered down the stairs. She snatched up her handbag and briefcase and left the station at the next thing to a run. The thought of Dan and his problems peeled away under the sharp edge of anticipation.

Dinner and dessert.

He'd promised.

_11_

HOW DID YOU dress for a seduction when you had to appear in public and eat dinner first?

Eve considered her closet for the fifth time since arriving home. After her shower, she'd done her makeup with special care and put her hair up in a twist decorated with one of Nana's mother's Art Deco diamond clips. The evening was a warm one, telling her that they'd all be wilted and sweaty when the blast furnace of summer actually hit. So with the temperature in the low eighties, velvet and anything satiny was out.

She fingered the red gauze blouse he'd said he liked. Unconsciously, she'd put on a bloodred lipstick that was a good match for it. Hey, why fight her instincts? She pulled the top on and cinched the wide sash ties into a big bow under her breasts, where it had the inevitable effect of drawing the eye to her cleavage.

No wonder Mitch liked it. Plus, this deep red was a good color on her. Now. Skirt. She chose a long black knit slit up both sides, and stepped into black stilettos that made her legs look much longer than they were.

Turning in front of the mirror, she nodded. The combination of the youthful top with her grandmother's diamonds was unique and fun—an image she worked hard to project on camera. Not to mention comfortable. When you were in the public eye as much as she was, comfort couldn't be overrated.

She decided against earrings—they'd only slow her down when she and Mitch were tearing each other's clothes off. Oh happy thought. And where was he, anyway? Seven-thirty had come and gone.

As if she'd conjured him up with the thought, the doorbell rang, and she clicked down the hall to answer it.

Damn, he looked good behind a whole lot of red roses.

Mitch held out the enormous bouquet. "Sorry I'm late. Apparently there's a shortage of these. I had to go to three places to make up a dozen. Can you believe that?"

Taking them from him, she buried her face in the fragile petals and inhaled their wildly romantic scent. "I can't believe you went to all that trouble."

"It's worth it. Between the bouquet and you, I'm speechless." He leaned over the flowers and kissed her.

His lips asked, "Do you feel the same way as you did two hours ago?"

And hers replied, "Oh yes. Just you wait."

When he pulled back, his eyes were dark and he couldn't seem to take his gaze off her mouth. "Are you sure you want to go out for dinner first?"

"If we don't go," she whispered, "we never will. And I hardly have a thing in the fridge."

He nodded as if he were trying to convince himself. "You're right. Ready?"

"Just let me do something with these flowers and get my wrap."

It seemed to Eve that dinner was less about the food than about scent and flavor and heat—and Mitch. She couldn't have said whether she ate pork or beef, but she knew what his hands looked like as they held fork and steak knife. The wine was a wonderful pinot noir—but she only knew that because he said it was the same color as her blouse.

Her senses—taste, touch, sight—seemed to be intensified, as though the addition of Mitch to her life made her experience it more deeply or more thoroughly. She'd been in love before—with Rafe in college in Florida, and then briefly Austin Taylor, a newscaster who had left CATL-TV just before the show had taken off. She'd thought she knew the signs, but they hadn't been anything like this.

She didn't love Mitch, she told herself as he handed her his steaming espresso to counter the sweetness of the exquisite crème brûlée. Love didn't work like that—didn't explode into being in the course of a week of business negotiations. But she was certainly a little bit *in* love with him, and the anticipation of what was to come was like frosting on the cake of a wonderful evening.

He hadn't even touched her outside of a hand on her waist as he guided her out of the restaurant and into the car. But her whole body was singing with need until, by the time they got to his hotel, she was as soft and moist as if they'd been kissing the whole way instead of driving.

"I hope you appreciate the extent of my self-restraint," he murmured in the elevator as they floated to the tenth floor. "I've managed to go two whole hours without throwing you down on the nearest table and ravishing you."

"Name the last time you heard anyone say 'ravish.'" Her tone teased. Her eyes promised that she'd let him do just that, if he wanted.

"You did." He pulled out his key as they walked, and unlocked a door about halfway down the corridor. "In a show last winter on the physics of the bra."

"I remember that one. Boy, did the ratings ever spike."

He ushered her in and closed and locked the door. "As of this moment, we are not talking business anymore." He slid the wrap off her shoulders and draped it over a chair. "Can I get you a small but criminally expensive drink from the minibar?"

"No," she whispered. "I've been waiting all night to kiss you properly."

"I've been waiting to kiss you *im*properly."

And then there was no more waiting. He turned and scooped her into his arms, his mouth coming down on hers. Her head fell back as she welcomed his lips, his tongue and the promise of complete possession later. Because that's what this kiss was—a promise of things to come.

She could hardly wait, and at the same time, she wanted this moment to last forever.

Oh, my, he tasted good. His tongue teased hers, and she met him halfway. He advanced, and she invited, until their kiss deepened into a conflagration of texture and desire. How was it possible that lips could be so soft and wooing, and a tongue could be so hard and suggestive?

Eve took every suggestion he made and turned it into a seduction until they were both gasping for breath.

Still holding her, he backed up until his knees met the mattress. He reached back and stripped the glossy coverlet off it with one hand.

"If we land on that thing, we'll slide right off it," he said, pulling her onto the crisp sheets.

"Good plan." She lay beside him and toed off her sandals. They dropped to the floor with a double clack. He reached down and tossed his shoes toward the closet door.

"Stop right there," she ordered softly. "I get to do the rest."

"Yes, ma'am."

"Very good." Leaning on one elbow, with the other hand she loosened his tie and whipped it off his neck and over one shoulder. "You sound like a real Southerner."

"When in Rome. Sure I can't help you with these buttons?"

"Absolutely not." She made short work of them, and obligingly, he lifted up so she could remove his shirt. "Mmm." She ran an admiring hand over his chest, feeling the mat of curly hair, springy with life. "You feel good."

"You look good. You wore my favorite blouse."

"A Southern lady always thinks of others." Her hand strayed down to his belly, slowly mapping the contours of his abs. *My, oh my.*

"Does a Southern gentleman think about what the lady has under her clothes?"

"I'm sure he does, but he would never, ever mention it." She debated whether she should explore the growing bulge in his trousers from under his waistband and belt, or through the fine wool.

"Okay." His voice was husky as he leaned over. "I won't say a word."

And he lowered his head to kiss the curve of her breast. His tongue swirled on her skin, tracing the plunge of her cleavage and working up the other side. It felt glorious, as though he were worshipping every inch of exposed skin.

"Have I told you lately how beautiful you are?" he whispered as he moved red gauze aside to expose the red lace of her bra. He ran his tongue under the scalloped edge.

"Not since yesterday," she managed.

"What terrible manners. I like your lingerie."

"I thought you might."

"Next time, don't wear any. Remember what I said before."

Did she ever. "You like to look."

"That I do. May I?" He pulled the edge of the cup down and exposed her nipple.

"Please, Mitch." She arched her back and moved as if to force herself into his mouth, but he pulled back.

"Not so fast. I want to look first."

The man was an expert at torture, but at the same time, it was tremendously exciting to be the focus of that hot gaze. He released the front catch and her bra sprang apart. And then, unexpectedly, he arranged the wrap front of her blouse over her naked breasts and pulled her up until they sat facing each other. The fabric was like a breath of sensation on her flesh, teasing her aching nipples while it hid them from his sight.

"Very nice," he breathed. "I can see your luscious nipples right through it."

Or not. Her breasts felt heavy with desire, and she was positive the nipples he loved had never been harder or more ready to be touched.

Slowly, he untied the bow in the front and unwrapped the blouse, pushing it and the bra off her shoulders. She kicked off her skirt, and he backed up against the headboard, where he pulled her into his lap so that she straddled him.

"Oh, my." She settled onto his erection, shielded by her wet panties and his trousers. Ooh. Very nice. Her breasts jiggled as she adjusted her position.

"Miss Best, I'm overcome by my need to taste your nipples. They are quite simply driving me mad. May I?"

If you don't, I'll scream. No, a Southern lady would never say that. "Please do." She resisted the urge to giggle and instead, rocked a little on his cock.

She settled her arms around his neck as he cupped her breasts in his hands and groaned with pleasure as her flesh filled them. "Lovely," he breathed. "So round. So firm." Then he lowered his mouth to her nipple and swirled his tongue around it before he suckled it. Delight darted along her veins as his clever tongue and teeth pleasured her, as he nibbled and sucked and licked his way from one to the other and back again.

"Miss Best," he said, his voice muffled against her skin, "I would like your permission to lick your nipples every day." He slid two fingers between their bodies, and she jumped with the sudden, unexpected pleasure as his fingers found their target. "And since we're on the subject, your clit, as well."

"Shall we write that into the contract?" she asked, and gasped as he hooked her panties with his thumbs and pulled them off. In return, she undid his belt and fly and yanked his trousers and boxers down, tossing them to the floor.

"If not the contract, then certainly your calendar." He pulled her into her former position, and she settled onto his naked cock as he gazed up at her. His mouth was swollen and his eyes glazed and dark with passion. He tongued a nipple, drawing it into his mouth and releasing it with a sound like a kiss. "I can't live a single day without at least looking at your magnificent breasts. Naked, of course. We'll need to specify that in writing." His hips rose under her, and she ground herself against him. "And making you come. In your office will be fine. On your desk, preferably, but I'll make do with the carpet if I have to."

"On my desk?" she asked weakly.

"Yes indeed. You can lie on it and I'll sit in your chair and eat you for lunch."

"Goodness," she whispered. "Lucky me."

"Miss Best, there's a condom in that wallet on the nightstand. Would you be so kind?"

In seconds she had it unwrapped and rolled down on him. He repositioned her above him and she sank onto the tip. A moan escaped her as she stretched to accommodate him.

"Miss Best," he ground out, cupping her breasts so that his thumbs abraded her nipples, "I can't wait any longer. Please use me ruthlessly for your pleasure."

She kissed him deeply and sank onto him, feeling his tongue slip into her mouth and his thick erection slide deep into her body. Feeling his hands on her breasts as she rose and fell in slow motion. Feeling his fingers slide between them to touch her clit and stimulate it, as slippery with her creaminess as it would be if indeed he did have her on her own desk, bringing her to orgasm with his tongue—

She shuddered as the pleasure detonated under his clever fingers, spreading through her body like a flash bomb. Her body contracted around him and he groaned. He gripped her waist and, even as she cried out with the magnitude of it, thrust into her again and again, his hips flexing against the mattress.

He drove into her a final time and gasped, and she clutched him tight with every internal muscle she knew how to use. "Eve!" he cried, and she felt his body shudder as his chest heaved with the effort to breathe.

And then they were spiraling down to the mattress again, twined around each other, holding on as if they were two survivors in a high sea.

"Yes," Eve said on a long sigh. "This is definitely going on my calendar."

12

EVE SAT ON a padded stool in the center of the set, facing the live audience. The spotlight felt hot on her scalp, but she was used to it—and besides, she never stayed on the stool very long. The electricity of the unpredictable usually goosed her off it within about five minutes—and goosed the ratings, too.

Atlanta loved these things.

Usually she did, too, but today her concentration was shot. The fact that she'd left Mitch's hotel room with barely enough time to skate home, change her clothes and get down to the station probably had something to do with it.

She'd had an Army shower—three minutes flat. It was impossible that she could still smell the scent of Mitch's aftershave, hours later. Impossible that her panties could still feel damp, or that her secret places could still be sensitive and slightly sore.

Something moved off to the side, and she saw the man himself take a seat at the far end of one of the right-hand rows.

What strings had he pulled to get a seat? People started lining up on the sidewalk outside at six in the morning. Getting in was a crapshoot. People who looked interesting, had interesting opinions or simply happened to be wearing a hat that their two PAs liked were admitted. Eve figured it was kind of like a New York club. It didn't matter how much money you had or who you knew. If the PAs nixed you, better luck next time.

Her music died away and she grinned at the camera. "Good afternoon, Atlanta—I'm Eve Best, and I'd like to keep this *Just Between Us*."

The crowd screamed and propelled Eve up off the stool. "We're swapping today with Friday, folks, in order to give you a two-part show. I want to talk about Understanding His Motives—Is What He Says Really What He Thinks?"

The studio rang with shouts and applause.

"For those of you brave enough to come up here and tell the truth—or not—you're going to be filmed, and then tomorrow Dr. Barbara Birdsall, who specializes in male/female communications, will analyze—" she put a hand on her hip and struck a pose "—just what exactly is goin' on."

The next half hour took all her ingenuity and stage management skills as two women took their boyfriends to task on live television. A husband made promises to his wife. A middle-manager type of about forty who was clearly skipping out on his day job talked about how difficult it was to get anything done in his all-female shop.

One of the angry women with the cheating spouse was a housewife who taught neighborhood women how to strip for their husbands or boyfriends. The crowd's response to her was so terrific that Eve made a mental note to get her booked for a show later in the month.

And then Cole was giving her the signal to wrap and their twenty-two minutes of live television was over. Town-hall days, while they might be unscripted, exhilarating free-for-alls, left Eve with a combination of a mental high and physical exhaustion. She always stuck around afterward, though, to thank the people who had been brave enough to come up on the stage. If they asked, she would usually pose for pictures and sign autographs.

As she did what she'd done hundreds of times before, though, a part of her mind focused on Mitch, zeroing in on him and holding him on the screen of her awareness as though she'd developed a silent radar overnight. And when the crowd finally thinned, she knew the moment he got up from his seat and made his way down to the front.

She steered the stripper housewife over to Nicole and turned to find Mitch near the false wall that backed onto the hallway to the lobby.

"Nice work," he said as he fell into step beside her. "It's like a three-ring circus. How do you keep everyone from killing each other?"

"This isn't Jerry Springer," she reminded him, ushering him up the stairs and into her office, and closing the door. "People are here to have fun, get something off their chests or contribute. I had a guy a couple of weeks ago get onstage as part of his civic duty. It was kind of funny because our topic was How Early Is Too Early for Sex Ed? He was a teacher. Took a day away from his classes because he felt so strongly that kids should be armed with information from day one."

"He should've had a talk with my mom," Mitch said. "She'd have preferred day billion. My dad wound up having to tell me about the birds and the bees when I was twelve."

What had he looked like at twelve? She'd bet those brown eyes and that narrow dimple at the side of his mouth had been just as effective on the girls in seventh grade as they were on her.

"Precocious child," she teased. "I'm happy you've made up for lost ti…mmm."

The rest of the word became a purr as he kissed it into oblivion. Mitch could make her forget every other sense she had except touch and taste. Her office disappeared in a slow swirl of sensation and anything else but this man and this kiss.

Several dazed minutes later, she surfaced and pulled back enough to breathe and to gaze into his face.

"Can I just move in here?" One corner of his mouth twitched as he spoke, and she kissed it.

"No. I'd never get any work done. And people would begin to suspect. Where would I hide you when I met with Dylan, for instance? You're too big to stash behind a potted plant."

"I'd have to go under your desk." He waved a hand at it. "Just think what I can do under there."

A slow flame kindled in her belly at the thought of it. An answering flame burned in his eyes—and the knowledge that if she so much as spoke the word, he'd crawl under there and do under it what he'd promised to do to her on top of it.

But before she could give in to temptation, a knock sounded on the door. "Eve?"

"Come on in, Dylan," she called.

She seated herself safely behind her desk, while Mitch leaned on the wall and gazed out the window.

"Oh good, you're both here." Dylan looked from one to the other. "Dan Phillips wanted me to set up an informal dinner for the three of you. Would today suit?"

Dinner? Eve frowned at Dylan. Dan wasn't a dinner kind of guy—informal or otherwise. And what had brought about this sudden burst of hospitality when he'd been so angry yesterday?

"What's going on, Dylan?" He always knew the hallway gossip. In fact, she counted on him when she needed to get the word out about something discreetly, or when she needed some clandestine detective work done.

But this time, her assistant shrugged, his brown eyes full of honest regret. "I don't know, boss. Word is he's pretty upset about you turning down the big networks—" he glanced at Mitch "—in favor of a smaller one, but you probably already knew that."

"*That* he told me," she admitted.

"And I saw both Ms. Roussos and Mr. Everard in the lobby this morning, a couple of hours apart. They didn't contact me to set up a meeting with you. So my guess is, they were meeting with Dan."

"Why would they do that if they're out of the running?" she wanted to know, turning to Mitch.

"They're coming back with a counteroffer," Mitch said flatly. "It'll be either money or location."

"Money won't do it, so it's probably location," she said. "What do you think, an offer to let us stay in Atlanta?"

"Would you take it?" He answered her question with one of his own.

"At first glance, no. We already agreed that CWB was the smarter way to go. That we'd risk less if we built our audience slowly."

"I'm glad to hear it," Mitch said simply. "I'm free for dinner, if you are."

"This ought to be interesting." She turned to Dylan. "Let Dan know we'll meet him over at Scarlett's at five. That's as informal as you can get."

"Will do." Dylan closed the door discreetly behind him.

Eve got up and joined Mitch at the window. She could feel the heat of the day radiating through the shaded, dual-pane glass.

"Tell me again we won't have to move if we go with CWB," she said. "That's not going to change."

"No, it's not," he said quietly. "The team stays in Atlanta, no matter what."

She nodded, and looked up at him. "This won't be pretty."

"Maybe not. But he wants to see us together. I'll back you up."

Outside of her team, it had been a long, long time since anyone had said anything like that to Eve. "Thanks. That means a lot to me."

After a pause, he said softly, "You've been on your own a long time, haven't you?"

Surprised at his perception, it took a second for her to shrug one shoulder in assent. "You get used to it."

"You must have had a good foundation as a kid. To learn to make your own decisions and develop the kind of confidence you have."

"My grandmother is responsible for that, I think. Being a teenager is never easy at the best of times, and when you lose your parents you feel like you're drifting in space, mostly. I don't remember junior high at all. Just vague images."

"I have junior high blocked out, myself. Sounds like your grandmother did a good job—I'm sure that was a bad time for both of you. But they say a person's character is formed by the time they're five. So your folks get some of the credit."

She glanced at him. "What brought this on? About my family?"

He shrugged and looked slightly embarrassed. "Just trying to figure you out. Learn what kind of influences made you the fascinating woman you are. And not just the TV host. The real woman."

The truth was, she'd allowed him to learn more about her in the week he'd been in Atlanta than almost anyone outside of her small, tight circle of friends. What did that say about him? And if it came to that, what did it say about her that she was opening up to him? There had to be more going on here than a fling with a time limit.

And was she ready for something like that? To get

into a relationship that brought both her sexuality and her maturity to the table?

That she'd never done before. She needed to stop asking herself these questions and make some decisions about herself.

"How long are you in town?" she asked suddenly.

"As long as I need to be. We still have to come to agreement on the terms of the contract, so I'll be around for a few days yet."

"Do you want to go somewhere with me on the weekend?"

"As long as it's not to a baseball game, I'm your man."

She grinned. "That's right. You're a hockey and soccer guy. Thank God. No, there's been something I've wanted to do ever since I came back to Georgia and I've never had the time or the guts to do it."

He looked confused. "The first I can understand, but not the second."

"You'd be amazed. Good. That's settled. Saturday, then."

"Uh, aren't you going to tell me what it is?"

She shook her head. "Not now. We have to go over to the deli to meet with Dan and it would take too long."

She hustled him out the door before she lost her courage and told him to forget she'd mentioned it. But deep inside she knew that by asking him to do this with her, she'd committed herself.

To a trip into her past.

And maybe into her future.

DAN PHILLIPS WAS waiting when they arrived at
Scarlett's, looking as though he were afraid the spindly
deli chairs would collapse and drop him on the tile.
Maybe it wasn't the best choice for a business meeting,
but it was informal. It was also busy and noisy and,
from what Mitch had learned, Eve's turf. All the staff
seemed to know her, and she'd hardly seated herself
when someone called out from the back, "The usual,
Eve?"

"Thanks," she'd replied, and then he and Dan had
had to play catch-up with the menus so their orders
would all arrive at once.

He didn't care. Food wasn't high on his list of priorities on the best of days. But if Eve had meant to make
Dan uncomfortable for this discussion—which he was
sure she hadn't because that wasn't her style—she'd
succeeded.

She didn't waste any time getting down to brass
tacks. "So, Dan, why don't we get started? Dylan didn't
say what you wanted to talk about."

Deliberately, Dan chewed and swallowed, then took a
sip of his cola, taking back control of the conversation.
After working with Nelson Berg, Mitch knew all the signs.

"I wanted to talk to you and our rep from CWB
together, since that seemed fair, about what's best for
the show," he began. "I'm not convinced that we're on
the right track."

"In what way?" Mitch asked. "I'll do whatever I can
to assure you CWB is the best choice."

"The thing that concerns me most is the advertising
revenue," Dan said bluntly. "It's a fact that the bigger

networks attract deeper pockets. That means they can attract advertising from cosmetics companies, car companies, pharmaceuticals. Not the local department store and Beulah's House of Curls."

"We have ad revenue from all those companies," Mitch assured them. "Maybe Kia instead of Chevy, and wineries instead of Coors and Bud Light, but that fits your demographic."

"Beulah's House of Curls was one of my first advertisers, Dan," Eve put in. "She stuck with us when things were really rocky in our first year. If you're thinking of cutting her out now that we're—"

Dan interrupted, and Eve looked taken aback. "If you go with CWB, she won't be able to afford the rates. But Beulah isn't relevant to this discussion. I still have reservations about partnering with a smaller network. I've been talking with Mackenzie and Chad, and they're willing to throw their hats back into the ring and negotiate about location."

Mitch exchanged a glance with Eve. Bingo.

"If you agree to go with one of them, they'll allow the show to stay in Atlanta."

"Will I get to keep my team?" Eve asked immediately.

"I can't guarantee that, but they do guarantee that any production people who come on board will be equal or better in terms of quality and experience."

Eve's eyebrows, which normally had a beautiful curve like the wings of a sea bird, drew together in a frown. "I don't want equal or better. I want my people. Cole, Zach, Nicole and Jane, in particular. And my two PAs and the junior segment producer."

Dan put his sandwich down and wiped his fingers. "Eve, I know you're not used to playing in the big pond, so let me give you some advice. You need to learn to give a little to get a lot. And in this case, we don't know if the network will replace some or all of your folks. But we do know that we can stay in Atlanta, so chances are good. If you appear to concede on that point, they'll be more likely to concede on location."

"So it's not a done deal, then." Mitch jumped on that like a duck on a june bug. "Whereas CWB has already given Eve a commitment."

"It's under very favorable discussion," Dan said, nettled. "SBN has told me that if it's a deal breaker, they'll concede."

"But it's not a commitment," Eve pressed him.

"It's on the table."

"That's not the same."

"Eve, listen to me," Dan said. "This strategy you're talking about with building slowly with a regional network—that may have worked in years past, but it won't work today. This is the MTV generation. People want a big splash, they want it now, and they want a lot of it. If you're going national, you have to go for the biggest deal you can get."

"No matter what it costs?" Mitch asked.

Dan eyed him, as if searching for sarcasm. But Mitch was perfectly serious. "I met with the other two networks in private, so inviting you along today was to give you the same opportunity to adjust your offer in light of what they're willing to do," the other man told him. "I'd hoped we could be objective about Eve's choices, but I see that allowing you to sit in on this meeting was a mistake."

"I disagree," Eve said at once. "I should have been in on those meetings, too. But I think you have more at stake here than I do, Dan. It seems to me you're the one having difficulty being objective, not me."

"You're not the only one with a career path." Dan's voice sounded muffled as he tried to keep his voice from carrying.

"That may be so, but it's not your career that the networks are buying," Mitch put in. "It's Eve's. We need to focus on the best thing for her and her team, and objectively, I believe that CWB is it. I disagree about your MTV philosophy. Eve's demographic isn't that generation. Her success has been regional, and building on that is the best way to go."

"I wouldn't be so quick to talk about objectivity, Mr. Hayes, when your relationship with Eve has been about as far from that as you can get."

Mitch sat back in his chair, unsure if the man meant what it sounded like he meant. "I beg your pardon?"

"Yes," Eve said with scathing politeness. "Clarify that for me, would you, Dan?"

The man shrugged and picked up his sandwich. "It just seems odd to me that the other network reps have been very aboveboard in their meetings with me, while you choose to meet with Eve alone, in nonbusiness settings. Aside from the fact that you seem to be cutting CATL-TV's management out of your discussions, it disturbs me that the way you spend your time with Eve can be, uh, too easily misconstrued."

"Speak English, Dan," Eve suggested, clearly trying to keep her temper.

"Meetings in the park, Eve?" he asked, eyebrows rising. "And at your home? Come on."

"I'll have my meetings wherever I want. We're talking business."

"If I were meeting with Mackenzie Roussos in my apartment, would you say that about me?"

"Yes. And I'd mind my own business, and so should you. Have you got somebody following me, or what?"

"I have sources all over town," he pointed out. "If one of the tabs happens to call me with a question about Eve Best's latest arm candy, it's my job to know."

"That comment was derogatory to Mitch," she snapped. "And you have no right to talk to a journalist about me. That's been our policy from day one."

"Times have changed," Dan replied.

Mitch decided it was up to him to step in before one of them said something that couldn't be taken back. "I think each of our positions is very clear," he said. "I recommend that we table this discussion. Eve will consider everyone's offer and let us know what she and her people decide. Isn't that right?"

He put all the appeal he could into his gaze, begging her not to lose it and back Dan into a corner he couldn't get out of without loss on both sides.

Eve pushed her sandwich away and got up. "That's fine. Excuse me, gentlemen. I don't mean to cut this short, but I have video to screen and a script to prep for Dr. Birdsall tomorrow. I'll talk to you both later."

She laid a hand on Mitch's shoulder, as if trying to

communicate to him that she wasn't angry with him. He saw Dan Phillips register the gesture and frown before she was out the door, leaving it swinging shut behind her.

13

EVE COULD ONLY be grateful that watching the video cut into segments for her by the show's editor required every ounce of her concentration. The script for their male/female communications show, which she'd been working on this morning, didn't need much support from her. She'd structured the show so that Dr. Birdsall's commentary on these video clips would be the highlight.

She was glad that for once, the focus wouldn't be on her.

Sitting in one of the station's three editing booths, she and Cole approved the segments they would send to Dr. Birdsall, which had been promised by 8:00 p.m. Try as she might, though, every time the editor finished a clip and saved it into its own file—"Cole, don't let me forget to follow up and see if Nicole got that stripper housewife booked"—the anger and guilt bubbled up out of the cracks in her concentration.

If she'd been alone, she could have fumed at Dan aloud. But as it was, she had to stuff him in a box in the back of her mind. She'd take him out later and yell at him in private—in her imagination.

Or better yet, she could call Mitch and they'd yell at him together, in absentia. Maybe she'd do that, as soon as she and Cole were finished. Any excuse to hear that voice one more time.

"Four clips, right?" The editor ran the digital counter under the last frame and clicked the mouse. "One for each five minutes?"

"I think so. If we keep them to two minutes each, that gives Dr. Birdsall time for her analysis and me time to elaborate. Plus a minute each for the opening mono-logue and my close."

"Have I told you lately how brilliant this idea is?" Cole watched the editor save the four clips up to the production server, where two of their five camera op-erators would run them at the times Eve had indicated in her script. "It's something new. I bet that you'll get a boatload of letters asking that the town halls be moved permanently to Thursday. The chance that an audience member can star in their own segment will be a big draw. Reality TV comes to Atlanta."

"We'll see. If the lines get any longer, we'll have to hire bouncers."

Cole thanked the editor for his work, and when the kid had made his escape, he opened an e-mail screen. "What's Dr. Birdsall's addy?"

She gave it to him, and watched him type a message letting the psychologist know where she could view the clips. When he hit Send, she glanced at the clock. Eight-fifteen. A little late to call Mitch. She'd make it an early night. Lord knew she could use it, after getting next to no sleep the night before.

Had it only been the night before? It seemed a week ago.

"Everything okay with you, Evie?" Cole asked, leaning back in his chair as the e-mail went off into cyberspace. "You seem…preoccupied."

What a sweetheart he was. He had his own problems with being a single dad, not least among them the fact that he'd had to arrange child care in order to stay here with her tonight. And still he could take the time to show her his concern, the way he had since the earliest days at the station when they'd both been green as beans.

"I am," she admitted. "I didn't mean for it to show, though."

"About the buyout? Or about…other things?"

"Both."

"I figured so." He stretched his big frame, making the chair squeak. Not for the first time, Eve wondered what kept him in this industry when he was so much happier bushwhacking around the wilderness or loading his kids and the dog into a canoe in the north woods. "Word in the halls is that Dan's got his panties in a twist about us choosing CWB."

"Word in the halls is right. But what's worse is that SBN and CBS have come back and said that they'll let us stay in Atlanta, too."

Cole lifted an eyebrow. "And this doesn't make us jump for joy because…"

"Because I don't think they mean it. I think it's a bait and switch to cut CWB out before any signatures go on paper."

He nodded thoughtfully. "Could be. From what you said, they seemed pretty adamant about New York in the beginning."

With a sigh, she said, "I have to admit this is getting to me. I thought we had a decision we could all be happy with. Now I have to call another meeting and present the new offer to everyone. And goodness knows how that will go. It's pretty hard to turn down more money plus staying here if that's all you see."

"I think Nicole sees the big picture. And Jane and Zach would, too. But yeah, it's still a risk." He paused. "Word in the halls didn't stop there."

"Oh?"

He grinned at her. "You have that innocent look perfected. It's me, remember?"

Someday, some lucky woman would convince this guy that she could be trusted. Eve looked forward to that day.

"I never forget," she said, smiling back. "Come on, out with it."

"It's kind of personal."

Obviously it was. It had probably gone around the station at the speed of light. "I can handle it."

"Word is that you and the CWB guy have a thing going on. That being the reason you want to go with them instead of the big guys."

"Is it, now?" Keeping something on the down low around here was like keeping M&M's in your desk. It wasn't a matter of if someone would find them, but when. "Are people saying he's romancing me to get the deal? Do they know how insulting that is?"

"I don't know, Eve. It seems too pat that he'd appear out of nowhere like this and sweep you off your feet, just when they need you on their roster."

"And *I'm* ripe for the picking, being totally inexperienced where good-looking men are concerned." Her tone dripped sarcasm, but Cole only reddened slightly. She had to give him credit. He wasn't ducking and running.

"You know that's not it. You have a good head on your shoulders—not to mention more knowledge about the subject than any ten women. Besides, God help any guy who hurts you. After you're done with him, the rest of us will run over his remains with the camera dolly."

"You think Mitch is going to hurt me? Are you giving me relationship advice, Cole?"

"No, I'm passing on the dirt is all. I thought you'd want to know."

"Well, if it should come up again, you can let the hallway gossips know that if—and I stress the *if*—there were anything between me and Mitchell Hayes, it would have occurred *after* the team agreed to the deal, not before."

"If?" Again that questioning eyebrow.

"So maybe there might be now. I don't know."

"No kidding." A slow grin, different from the previous one, spread across his face. "Good for you, Evie."

"It's bad, isn't it?" she asked quietly. "What they're saying."

"Who cares? If the guy honestly makes you happy and he's on the up-and-up, it's nobody's business. I'd be careful, though. You don't want to compromise the deal."

"I'm not giving anyone any ammunition. We don't

see each other very much, and when we do, we keep it private."

"Except for those lunches in the park."

"Where we sit at opposite ends of a hard bench and talk. Good grief, are people saying we're at it like rabbits under a bush?"

He laughed, the sound burying itself in the egg-carton walls of the editing booth, which was part of the recording suite. "I wouldn't go that far, but there was much interested speculation. Not everyone is suspicious. Some of us are happy for you, Eve. We think you work too much."

Maybe that was true. "Y'all will be happy to know I'm not working on the weekend, then."

"Got something fun planned? The girls and I are taking the boat out."

"I was thinking of Mirabel." At his puzzled look, she elaborated. "It's a plantation house south of Social Circle." She hesitated and then decided to go on. This was, after all, the man she trusted day in and day out with her public self. Why shouldn't she trust him with a glimpse into her private self? That's what she planned to do with Mitch, right? "A hundred years ago, my family used to own it."

Now both eyebrows rose. "You're from a plantation family? How did I not know this? On what side?"

"My dad's. Bests farmed Mirabel for something like a hundred years, until my grandpa lost it in the sixties. Couldn't pay the mortgage or the taxes or something. I don't really know. I've never been there."

"Why don't you have Dylan do some research on it? He's good at that stuff."

"No." Eve dropped her gaze to the keyboards behind Cole. "I'd rather keep it just between us, if you don't mind." A second too late, she realized what she'd said when he grinned again. "And don't even think about putting that up on the board as an idea for the show, because the answer is no."

"Aw, come on. It's perfect. The hidden history of our favorite celebrity."

"It's personal. Never you mind."

"You'll let me know if you decide otherwise?" He got up and picked his khaki jacket up off the back of his chair.

"You'll be the first." She let him usher her out and walk her back to her office, where he waved and headed down the hall toward the stairs. Cole Crawford never used an elevator if he could help it.

Ha. That would be the day that she made an episode all about her discovery of her family—or not. Mirabel, she'd discovered during a couple of Google searches, was open to the public on the weekends, but nobody lived there now. During the week, one of the charity trusts held events in the drawing room and had an office upstairs. Chances were low she'd discover anything about her ancestors there, but she wanted to check it out anyway.

It was something to share with Mitch. With him, she was discovering all kinds of things about herself. Maybe she'd discover something more if they did this together.

EVE HAD BARELY opened her eyes Saturday morning when the phone next to her bed rang. It had to be Mitch. None of her friends would think of calling before ten o'clock on a weekend unless they were hoping for a ruptured eardrum.

"'Lo?"

"Oh, no, I woke you." His voice was as deep and dark as corn syrup, and just as sweet.

"No, you didn't. But not by much." She yawned, and then caught herself. How rude was that?

But he chuckled. "I'm only sorry I wasn't there to do it in person. I called both your numbers last night but got no answer."

"You should have left a message. I wanted to call you, but I got home pretty late." She stifled another yawn, and stretched instead. "I wondered who those hangups were. Are you coming over?"

"Would you think I was a dork if I said I was parked outside?"

"What?"

Mitch laughed and hung up. With a thrash of her legs, she kicked the sheet off and dashed into the bathroom. A quick swipe of toothpaste was all she had time for before she heard him knock on the door.

Hair! Three licks with the hairbrush made it lie flat, at least, and then she had to answer the door or he'd think she was putting him off.

Naturally, he looked good enough to eat in a pair of soft, faded jeans and a light shirt open over a white T-shirt. His hair was loose and tousled, as though he'd been driving with the windows open.

Sigh. She had no idea where this was going or how long it would last—or even if it could, considering the fact that people were talking already. But she had today—and she'd promised herself she'd enjoy the heck out of it.

"My dream come true." He stepped inside and slid both hands around her waist.

"Right," she said. "Lucky for you I had toothpaste handy."

"Lucky for me all the way around." He leaned in and explored the sensitive skin under her ear. "You are *finally* not wearing a bra or some miracle of modern engineering."

She slept in a tank top and a pair of seersucker draw-string pajama bottoms that were probably wrinkled to a fare-thee-well. But from the heat building in his eyes, Mitch wouldn't have cared if she slept in chain mail, as long as there wasn't a bra under it.

With a delicious sense of her own power, she backed out of his reach. "Just let me get dressed."

"Oh, no, you don't." He followed her down the sunny hall, stalking her like a big, casual cat.

"No, really. No Southern lady would ever greet a guest in such dishabille." She reached her bedroom door and pushed it open with one hand. "I'll only be a—"

With a growl, he tackled her, and she shrieked with laughter as she landed on her back on her bed. He rolled her on top of him, both his arms around her waist, and she kicked and slid off, landing on her side and wriggling away.

He grabbed her again from behind and this time he pinned her down with one leg thrown over hers. Breathless with laughter, she pretended to struggle as he pushed her hair aside and nuzzled the nape of her neck.

Shivery kisses, she thought with delight as goose bumps prickled on her shoulders. And that wasn't all. Her skin seemed to come alive in response to the touch of his mouth and her nipples hardened as well.

A sound of satisfaction rumbled in his throat. Looking over her shoulder, he eased his grip on her waist and cupped a breast with one hand. And oh, it felt good to be fondled and shaped like this, as if her body had been waiting for his hands ever since that mad rush out of his hotel room yesterday morning.

He caressed her shoulders and bare arms, and slid his hands down to the hem of her top. With a whisper of fabric, he pulled it over her head and tossed it away. She rolled to face him and did the same with his shirt. "It'll get wrinkled," she whispered in explanation as it landed partly on the floor and partly over the arm of the wicker chair next to the window.

"Like I need an excuse to get naked with you." He toed off his tennis shoes. After he snagged a condom out of the pocket, his jeans followed the shirt through the air to the chair.

She wiggled out of her pj bottoms and then his big body lowered itself to hers. His hips fit into the cradle of her thighs, forcing them apart, before he turned his attention to her breasts. Her eyes slid closed with delight as he stroked pleasure from her skin with his tongue, swirling and tasting and sucking. Her nipples ached with impatience as he took his time getting there, as though he were saving the best for last.

"So hard for me," he whispered, his lips hovering an inch away from the aching peaks. "So sexy."

"Mitch." She arched her back, but he drew away, teasing. "You know how sensitive I am. Don't make me wait."

"I want a promise first."

There could be only one thing he could torture her for like this. "All right," she said, her breath coming fast. "No bra today."

"That's my girl." His voice was rich with satisfaction as at last he lowered his mouth and gorged himself on her. She marveled at the delight he took in her body, at the sweet fire he could ignite inside her with only his eyes and his mouth. His tongue swirled over her areolae and the slick abrasion made her moan. When he tugged, she gasped, and when he nibbled, it drove her mad.

Who would have thought that the part of her that gave him the most pleasure would be the part that felt pleasure the most?

This man is made for you.

Oh, no, she couldn't think that way. She couldn't think at all, because now he was rolling on the condom and positioning himself between her legs. And she couldn't wait another second. She was so ready—so wet and soft, her body demanding his.

Eve pulled up her knees to give him easier access and pulled him toward her. "Now," she gasped. "I need you now."

In a single stroke, he plunged into her, and she shrieked. Again and again he drove home, his gaze locked on her face and yet turned inward as though his own pleasure were taking over his senses. She slipped her hand between their bodies and touched herself, finding the center of her pleasure and adding the stroking of her fingers to the rhythm of his body.

"Eve—" he choked.

A red explosion of pleasure erupted inside her and she clenched around him like a vise, shuddering and making incoherent little cries. He cried out, too, and found his release as he rocked into her one last time.

His skin felt damp and hot under her clutching fingers as he collapsed onto her in a spent heap. Her bed folded them both into its soft embrace.

This man is made for you.

Maybe. Maybe not. But one thing was for sure.

The people at CATL-TV couldn't possibly be right about him. No one could make love like this and have an ulterior motive.

No one.

14

ONCE WAS NOT ENOUGH.

Or twice, because it hadn't even been an hour and he wanted her again. Maybe making love to Eve three times a day would satisfy him.

Mitch watched her strap herself into the Lexus and swallowed. She'd kept her promise, and the only question was how long he could control himself before someone caught him staring—or worse, touching.

He must have been crazy to ask her to do this.

She wore cargo pants that came just below her knee and rode low on her hips. A little strip of bare skin showed between the waistband and her top, not enough to be vulgar but just enough to draw the eye and tease.

And talk about teasing. She hadn't worn the red gauze number, because his eyes and his brain would have fried within a block. But she wore a cotton camisole that looked like it had come out of some Victorian lady's wardrobe. It fastened down the front with tiny pearl buttons, and scooped low in the neckline, a narrow lace ruffle framing cleavage that was truly spectacular.

He was a goner.

And if he caught any other guys staring at her, he'd bite off their heads.

"So. Where to?" He pulled out of her driveway and headed for I-20, which was one of the reference roads he'd memorized. In every city he scouted in, he scoped out the two main freeways. That way, he never felt lost, which meant he never felt out of control.

As for being alone in a lot of strange places, he'd gotten used to it. Came with the territory.

Eve pulled a piece of paper out of her sleek leather backpack. He caught a glimpse of a sun hat and a digital camera tucked away in there, as though she'd come prepared for an excursion. An adventure.

"I printed a map before I left the office last night," she said. "Head east and turn south at Social Circle. The plantation is about fifteen miles south and then east again."

Following her map, it didn't take long before the Lexus slowed to a stop at a wrought-iron sign that swung next to the country road.

"Mirabel," Eve read. "Est. 1858. Property of the Ashmere Trust. That's the same people who organized the benefit we went to last week."

"I have fond memories of that benefit," he said. "Personal reasons aside, they seem to do good work."

He pulled into a driveway that was more like a lane, winding off into a tangle of trees and some kind of voracious ivy that covered the ground. Eve sat forward in her seat, gazing intently out the window.

"Recognize anything?" he asked. "Any ancestral memory?"

With a flash of a smile, she said, "I'm interested in everything, that's all. It's a shame we're too late for the rhododendrons."

He was a desert rat, transplanted to the concrete jungle. All the trees and shrubs looked pretty much the same to him, but if she said those tall bushes with the dark leaves were rhododendrons, he'd take her word for it.

And then he forgot about the plants. He was too busy watching Eve's face from the corner of his eye as the house came into view.

"Wow," she breathed.

It wasn't your standard Old South icon, with marble pillars and tall windows. Mirabel had been a working farm, and its spreading, clapboard lines showed it. But still, its two stories and eight front windows looked welcoming, as did the wide verandah, where Mitch had no doubt some previous generations of Bests had taken an afternoon whiskey and played games.

As they got out of the car in the parking lot, the front door opened and a petite woman of about seventy stepped out. "Are you folks here for the eleven o'clock tour?" she called.

Eve exchanged a glance with Mitch. "Uh, no, but we'd love to take it," she said.

"Come right this way. My name is Adele Pierce and I'm a volunteer docent at Mirabel."

They shook hands and Adele ushered them into the front hall. Then she looked Eve full in the face. "Pardon me for saying this, but you look terribly familiar. Have we met before?"

Eve smiled, and Mitch realized she probably got that same question every time she went to the grocery store. Look what had happened at the mall last weekend.

"I have a show on CATL-TV called *Just Between Us*. Do you watch it?"

The woman shook her head, eyeing Eve as much as politeness would allow. "No, I don't have a television. My husband tells people I was born late…by about a hundred years. He was in the computer business, but I've never even turned one on. Never mind. It will come to me. It always does."

Mitch waited for Eve to tell the docent that she was a member of the Best family, but when Adele showed them into a room that she explained was one of the parlors and Eve still said nothing, he concluded she didn't want to go public about her interest in her family.

When Adele led the way across the hall to what was obviously a formal dining room, Mitch leaned in and whispered, "Not going to out yourself to our guide?"

Eve shook her head. "How weird would it look? I mean, what old-line Southerner doesn't know everything about their family heritage, right down to the last twig on the family tree? Nana told me some stuff about my mom and dad's generation when she was alive. And yes, I got the tour of Uncle Roy's family photos, but as far as the family that lived here, I know next to nothing."

"So you're a tourist in your own backyard, huh?"

"Literally."

Adele stopped next to the fireplace, where a massive mantelpiece was held up by a pair of Art Nouveau nymphs. "The house has had a number of renovations," she explained, "the most extensive of which took place in 1910 after Artimas Best made a killing on the stock market." She ran an affectionate hand over the lines of a nymph's flowing tunic. "This mantel, which even I have to admit looks completely out of place in a structure that was essentially a farmhouse, was imported from England. And over it you'll see the wedding portrait of Artimas and Evalyne Best. Evalyne was one of the Eden sisters, who were the belles of their generation. She married Artimas in 1903."

Dutifully, Mitch looked up at the black-and-white photo, which was a little blurred with age.

And he blinked. Looked from Evalyne to her... what? Great-great-granddaughter? And back again. There was the sensual mouth and the wide-set eyes. Evalyne's hair was pulled up and poufed out in Gibson girl style, but it was dark like Eve's, and while she was nearly lost to sight in a cascade of ruffles, there was no mistaking the corseted hourglass figure.

He couldn't tell if Eve was having the same sense of déjà vu. She stood on the Turkey-red carpet, gazing silently at her ancestors as if they were a puzzle she'd figure out if they just gave her long enough.

Mitch glanced at Adele, who had obviously made the same discovery he had.

"Miss, if you don't mind me saying so, I now know why you seem so familiar. I've been looking at your face for about nine months, that's why."

Eve turned to her. "My face?"

The older woman gestured at the portrait. "You're a

dead ringer for Evalyne Best. Are you a member of the family, by any chance?"

Mitch waited for Eve to fib and end the odd moment with a suggestion that they move on with the tour.

"I am," she said instead. "My name is Eve Best."

Adele put a hand on her heart. "Mercy sakes. You don't say."

"And from what I can figure out, that lady up there is my great-great-great-grandmother."

"Great… Let's see now." Adele did some figuring in her head. "Artimas and Evalyne had a boy and two girls. The girls married men from Savannah—brothers, they were—and moved away, but the boy stayed on to run the family business, which was a savings and loan outfit until the crash of twenty-nine. He had two boys, Cecil and Merlon."

"My grandpa was called Cecil."

"Well, there you go. Cecil had two boys, as well. Your dad must have been Gibson, because your Uncle Roy is on the board of the Ashmere Trust and I know both his girls." Eve nodded. "I was so sorry about your parents, dear. Such a tragedy."

"It happened a long time ago. But thank you."

"When you're as old as me, 'a long time ago' is relative," Adele said with some asperity. Then her voice softened. "So you've come back to Atlanta and have a television show, do you? I'm glad to hear it. Your aunt and uncle will be glad you're home, too."

"They are. Do you know them well?"

"Roy and my husband did some business together. A start-up, I think you call it. I never pay much attention to that kind of thing. It's much more interesting to learn about lace-making patterns and how to preserve quilts, in my opinion."

Eve laughed. "My aunt might agree with you. She tried to teach me to sew when I was a kid, but I was never very good at it."

"Your mother wasn't, either, poor thing. But lands, she was a beautiful woman. Talk about the belle of her generation. The family had fallen on hard times by the time she married into it. Your grandpa had to give up this property and they moved to a place in town when your dad and uncle were boys. In fact, I babysat them when I was a teenager. Now, *that* was a long time ago."

Mitch had to smile at her truthful but self-deprecating humor. Then she took Eve's elbow and led her to the main staircase in the hall.

"I really shouldn't do this, but since you're a member of the family, I'd say you have the right. There are some pictures and things upstairs that you might be interested in."

As they followed her up the staircase to the second floor, Mitch asked, "There are family pictures still here? Didn't they go when the family moved away?"

"The originals did." Adele waved a hand at the open rooms they passed. "These are the children's bedrooms. The photos are in the master bedroom, here at the end. When the trust took this place over, Roy Best gave permission to make copies of some of the portraits. The walls were bare, you see."

She led them into a huge room with ten-foot ceilings

and narrow windows that had to be six feet high. A canopied bed occupied one end, and a fireplace the facing wall. On the wall to the left of the door, more portraits hung in a cluster. Some of them, Mitch was sure, had to have been taken right after the invention of the camera.

"Here's Evalyne and the children," Adele said, pointing. "That's Cecil and his bride in the forties, just before he went off to England to fight in the war. And Eve, here's your mother and dad and your Uncle Roy. This was taken in the early seventies, I think."

"Belle of her generation is right," Mitch murmured to Eve. "I see where you get your looks."

"Not really." Eve studied the picture. "I might have her chin, but not much else. I'm surprised how much I look like Evalyne, though. My niece Emily does, too. She's fourteen."

"Roy's daughter?" Adele asked. "She does, now you mention it. It's the mouth and the eyes. Very distinctive. Evalyne was said to be a woman of, shall we say, a very firm character, too."

"That definitely describes my niece," Eve said with a smile. "Much to her mom's dismay."

"You, too," Mitch put in. "Not every woman could step onto a set and have a couple of hundred people in the palm of her hand within a few minutes."

Eve shrugged modestly, then turned to Adele. "I don't suppose there's a copy of this picture, is there? I would love to have one. I don't have many photos of my parents, and I've never even seen this one."

Adele's forehead creased as she thought. "I'm not

sure. Let me check in the office, all right? Feel free to ramble around. I'll come and find you."

Mitch waited until he heard Adele's footsteps on the stairs before he spoke. "I hope she finds a copy for you. If she doesn't, maybe you can ask your relatives for one."

"Nana didn't have it in her belongings when she died." Eve's voice sounded puzzled. "I hardly have any pictures of my family. It's strange, don't you think?"

He considered this. "Maybe they were all sent to your uncle when your folks passed away."

"Not even when I was a kid," she said, as if he hadn't spoken. "You'd have expected my parents to talk about the family like Adele does. All proud, with tons of detail that would bore to tears anyone who wasn't related. But they never did. And the only pictures I remember seeing were Nana's wedding photo and the ones I got of myself at school."

"Some people just aren't pack rats." What was she getting at? And what was with that odd, tense look around her mouth, as though she'd turned over a rock and found something ugly under there? "I wouldn't upset yourself over it."

"I'm not upset. I'm confused. This isn't the first time I've wished I could ask my mother questions about her life. Like this picture, for instance."

He looked at it again. Three people. Two guys in lightweight suits with shaggy hair, a young woman with long hair parted in the middle, wearing platform shoes and a miniskirt.

"What about it?"

She pointed at one of the men. "That's my dad, the blond guy." Her finger moved to the other man, the one with his arm around the young woman. "And that's my Uncle Roy."

"Okay." He let his voice rise a bit, giving her room to go on.

"So why does my Uncle Roy and not my dad have his arm around my mom?"

Why did anybody do anything? "Maybe they were goofing around for the camera. Maybe Uncle Roy was trying to get your dad's goat or something. I have friends like that. Everything's a competition, a contest to see who can one-up the other."

"They look like they're together, don't they?"

"Huh?" Mitch blinked at the picture.

"Look how he's holding her. How his hand is on her waist, how she's snuggled up against him. A Southern girl from a good family, even in the seventies, would only let a boy hold her like that if they were serious about one another. Engaged, even. And look at my dad. He isn't smiling, but the other two are."

"And this means…?"

Her shoulders drooped. "I don't know what it means. All I know is that I've never seen this picture before, and there isn't one like it at my uncle's place."

"It could be packed away. My mom has boxes of old family pictures in albums, stacked in the closet under the stairs."

She glanced at him. "You probably noticed that all the family pride missing in my folks came out in my Uncle Roy in spades. If it was there, I'd have seen it, trust me."

Mitch heard Adele coming up the stairs, slower than she'd gone down them. A lady would have to be in good shape to act as docent around this place. No elevators.

"I still think you're reading something into it that isn't there."

She would have answered, but Adele came in holding a photograph in a plastic sleeve. "Well, this is a funny thing. Good for you, Eve, but funny all the same."

Eve took the photo and turned it over. "Oh?"

There was nothing written on the back.

"This is the original," Adele said. "It must be a mistake. Roy said that all the photos he donated to the trust were copies, except Artimas and Evalyne's wedding picture. That one's the real thing."

"Adele, did you know Roy and my dad? When they were teenagers, I mean. Like in this picture."

Adele, who up until now had been a fountain of facts and knowledge, dried up like the arroyos of Mitch's childhood in the summer. She cocked her head.

"Oh, there they are now, dears. The tour group that was supposed to have been here at eleven." She patted Eve's arm and ushered them out into the gallery. "You keep that photo, Eve. And you might want to check with your uncle and let him know we've returned an original. Feel free to poke around the grounds. I'd better hustle, or I'll never get them rounded up. People always think they can treat these houses the way they do their own."

Her voice faded as she clattered down the stairs, and

in a moment they heard her greeting the group. The buzz of a busload of people filtered up through the floor.

"Ready to go?" he asked. "Or do you want to look around?"

"No, I'm ready." Her voice was flat. Preoccupied. "But I'll be back. That woman was hiding something, and I'm going to find out what it is."

15

MAYBE MITCH WAS RIGHT. Maybe she was making too much out of a silly photograph. So two teenagers were cuddling. What did that mean? Teenagers cuddled all the time. It was the seventies, for heaven's sake. Just because her mom was cuddling with the wrong boy…

Wrong in whose opinion? Yours?

Maybe she'd dated Roy at one time and then decided that Gibson was The One after she'd graduated from college. Then why had Adele changed the subject so fast?

Eve hadn't been coaxing secrets out of guests four days a week, nine months a year for three years for nothing. She could spot a diversionary tactic a mile away—especially from a person who wasn't used to lying.

Eve pulled out her phone while Mitch stood in the eerie blue light in front of the windows of the dolphin tank at the aquarium. He was lost in a completely appealing, childlike wonder at the swooping and darting of the creatures.

"Dylan," she said when he answered, "I need you to do something for me on the qt."

He didn't even remind her that it was Saturday and he would have been completely within his rights to ignore her number on his digital display. "Sure. What's up?"

"I need you to get the home number of a docent who works at a plantation called Mirabel. Ever heard of it?"

"I've been there, yeah."

"You have?"

"My senior thesis was on representations of slave culture in the cinema. I've been to every place open to the public within about fifty miles of Atlanta."

No kidding. The things she was learning about people this weekend. "You probably talked to this lady, then. Her name is Adele and she's a volunteer with the Ashmere Trust."

"So you need home phone and address?"

"Just phone. I think she has some information for me, but I want to talk to her in private."

"Am I doing this clandestinely or as a rep of the show?"

"Use whatever method gets you that number."

"Copy that, boss. I have thumbscrews and cuffs in my date book. Agent Moore out."

With a smile, she hung up. She'd lobbed him some pretty weird requests since he'd come to work for her, and only once had he come up empty-handed. Of course, as it turned out, that particular member of the state senate had been arrested for shoplifting shortly afterward, so maybe it was just as well she hadn't had him on the show.

It took Dylan less than half an hour to call her back. "I've got your number," he said without preamble. "Got a pen?" He dictated it, and she wrote it on the notepad she kept in her handbag for this kind of thing.

"How'd you get it? Or should I not press you to reveal your sources?"

"It was easy," he said with a touch of pride. "I just explained to the girl at the trust's switchboard who I was and hinted that Adele might be on the scope for the show, and she was happy to give me her phone number. She probably would have given me the lady's address and all the names of her kids, too, but I stopped her in time."

Eve thanked him and disconnected. Now what should she do? Call Adele and arrange a meeting so she could force out of her whatever she was hiding? Or come at it in a more circuitous way and hope she let something slip?

Ha. Adele was a Southern lady. No manipulation would work on her. Honesty was the best approach.

"Have you been here so many times that you're bored silly?"

Mitch ambled up to her, his presence like a breath of air in the stifling confusion of her own thoughts.

"No, actually, I've never been here. It's kind of fun being a tourist in your own town."

"Forgive me for noticing, but you've spent more time on the phone than you have looking at the fish."

Speaking of honesty…

"I'm still bugged about that photo. I had Dylan track down Adele's home number so I can talk to her about it some more."

"Seems to me you'd be better off talking to someone in the family, like your grandmother or your uncle," he said reasonably. "Up until today, you never even heard of Adele."

"I'm going to do that, too."

"Are you sure you want to?" He took her hand and began to walk slowly toward the exit. "I mean, look at it from their point of view. You turn up on their doorstep asking a bunch of questions about a casual photo taken thirty years ago. All weirdness aside, how can it matter now?"

She exhaled, a long breath that acknowledged he was probably right. "I know. I can't argue that. Maybe it's just some compulsion inside me to connect with the past."

"Brought on by what?"

She glanced at him. Was the timing right? "I don't know. Maybe because I've spent the last couple of weeks thinking about the future."

"I hear you. I have to admit this deal is consuming most of my waking hours, too."

Now, what had happened here? She'd given him a classic opener to have a conversation about whether this was only a fling, or whether it could be something more, and he'd sent it swerving back to her. She didn't want to talk about business. If the truth were told, she was sick of thinking about the lawsuit and the station and the show and everybody's expectations.

Eve wanted to talk about *them.* She'd spent the last three years talking about relationships, while her personal life was as bare as a winter field. So how long could a person talk about something without really experiencing it?

If she were really honest with herself, maybe she'd been happy that way. If you became an expert on something, you could control it. You could live it in a surface kind of way, without risking your emotions and your vulnerabilities. The time had come to delve below the surface. To experience something so deeply that it might change her forever.

A deeply frightening thought.

But a challenge, too. And who had learned to be good at dealing with those over the last three years?

"I didn't mean the deal. I meant my personal future." She took a breath and plunged, feeling like one of those dolphins landing in the deep end of the tank. "And yours. Do you mean to tell me you haven't spent your waking hours thinking about me?"

As they went outside, the late afternoon heat clamped down on them like a smothering blanket. Eve hurried her steps as they made their way back to the car.

"Let me rephrase that," Mitch said. "Thinking about this deal means thinking about you. At night I dream about you. I wake up aroused, which means I start the day thinking about you. I've come to the conclusion I must be some kind of obsessive personality."

Well, there was nothing wrong with that. This was more like it.

"Have you given any thought to what happens when the deal is done?" she asked carefully. "About where this affair of ours might be going? Or if it's going anywhere?"

He pulled onto the freeway and she realized he was taking her back to her place.

Ooh. Maybe they could shower the sweat of the day away. Together. She had some beautiful European soap that would suds up nicely and—

"Are you always this forthright?" he asked.

"I like to be honest. I think we fell into this out of sheer sexual chemistry, but the more I do goofy things with you like going to the aquarium and the mall, the more I like being around you."

"I like being around you, too. And I really like being in bed with you."

"Yes, I noticed that you're taking me home."

"Only to drop you off, I promise. I'd like to go back to the hotel, grab a shower and take you someplace nice to eat before I take you to bed." That grin and those eyes were so wicked that Eve felt her body respond with enthusiasm.

"Any suggestions?"

What a beautiful mouth he had. And what a skillful tongue. Those alone were worth taking a risk for. "About what?" Maybe she could convince him to skip the hotel and have his shower at her place.

"Eve," he teased. "Focus. About food."

"Oh. Sure. Southerners love to eat, remember. It's just a matter of picking a place." It took them nearly the whole way home to settle on a restaurant, with Eve thinking all the while about a way to steer the conversation back to what she really wanted to discuss: themselves.

Finally she concluded there was nothing for it but to dive right in. "Are you sure you have to go back to your hotel?"

"Patience," he said as he pulled into her driveway. "Anticipation adds spice."

"Is that so." She watched him put the car into Park

and then leaned in for a kiss. "How long will you make me wait?"

Ha. There was a reason she'd worn this white cotton confection. A girl used the gifts she was given. She'd seen him heroically keeping his eyes on her face while they'd been rambling through public places today. Even though he'd asked her to be a little risqué for him, he was too much of a gentleman to do more than sneak an occasional peek. And she was happy about that. She had no desire to be embarrassed in public.

But now they were in private—or as private as her driveway would allow. As she leaned over, her plunging neckline gaped away from her skin, giving him a view of her lush curves.

"Guh," he managed.

"Come inside," she whispered against his lips, taking his hand and holding it tented over one breast. "Anticipation is overrated."

He made a low sound in his throat and kissed her deeply, his tongue thrusting against hers the way his body had earlier. The heat of his hand burned right through the fragile fabric as he fondled her, caressing the nipple with his thumb in a slow rhythm that made her squirm.

She had him. No man could say no after an invitation like this.

When he finally lifted his head, his eyes were black with desire, and he was breathing as heavily as she.

"You don't play fair," he rasped.

"I'm not playing at all. I want you *now*," she told him, her lips a promise against the underside of his jaw. "I don't want to wait until you get back."

"Neither do I," he admitted, "but I have to. My boss called. I didn't answer it at the aquarium, but I need to, soon. Otherwise he'll keep calling, and I'll go insane. I don't want to be crazed when I make love to you."

"Call him from here."

"The documents he wants to talk about are all at the hotel. I promise I'll be back in two hours, max."

He was as dedicated to his job as she was. Up until now, she'd have admired that. But her ideas were changing. She smiled, knowing when she was beaten.

At least there was a bright side, she thought as she waved goodbye and then turned to let herself into the house. If anticipation added spice, she was going to be as hot as a Thai chili by the time he got back.

NELSON BERG MAY have been a mediocre executive, but his timing was superb.

Superbly *lousy*.

Mitch cursed him, his job, CWB and all its affiliates all the way back to the hotel, which meant his emotions were a roiling soup of aggravation and sexual frustration when he opened the door to his room. Not the best frame of mind in which to talk to the man who could pull the plug on his career as easily as he could advance it.

Mitch took a shower to give himself time to calm down. When he came out, feeling clean at least, if not calm, his cell phone was already sounding the message alarm. He sighed. Nelson was as predictable as…well, hot weather in Atlanta.

He hit Reply To Last Caller and opened his briefcase, where the terms of the acquisition were laid out in a deal memo.

"What took you so long?" Nelson barked without so much as a hello.

"Most of a major metropolitan center was between me and this paperwork. I came back to the hotel to call."

"And what were you doing that far from your briefcase?"

"Nelson," Mitch said patiently, "it's Saturday. I know the days of the week have no meaning for you, but try to imagine a life where leisure time occurs once in a while."

"I tried to reach you yesterday, but you didn't reply then, either. If you're on the network's dime, Hayes, you'd better make yourself available."

"I turned my phone off during the taping yesterday. Must've forgotten to turn it back on again. I tell you, Nelson, this show is a gold mine. Eve came up with a new twist on the town-hall segment this week where audience members participated and then were analyzed the next day by a professional."

"Yeah, I saw it. What'd she have, a scheduling conflict with the talking head?"

Mitch pulled the phone away from his ear and stared at it, then put it back. "So, what can I do for you, now that we've connected?"

"I met with the executive committee this week, like I told you."

"You were going to let them know that Eve was signing on, the show was staying in Atlanta, and she would be able to keep her team." He glanced at the deal memo, where each point was laid out.

"Yeah. So about that."

Something in his voice caused a cold dart of apprehension to shoot through Mitch's belly. "Yes?"

"You know how NBC has Leno and CBS has Letterman?"

Was there anyone in the country who didn't? "Yes."

"The executive committee thinks that Eve has the potential to go national on that level. Instead of this daytime TV thing, they think she should do late-night. Dr. Phil and Oprah and the soaps pretty much have daytime wrapped up in the big markets, so CWB is looking to establish itself in the late slot."

Mitch took a deep breath. "Have they considered they'll lose Eve's primary demographic? Those viewers who tune in during the day aren't going to stay up until eleven."

Nelson started to say something, but Mitch cut him off. "And what about our plan to grow slowly? Eve totally bought into that. It was our primary differentiator over SBN and CBS. Which, by the way, aren't going to propose she go late-night. They want her for the daytime, where she's been successful. You run the risk of her backing out and choosing them. You know that, right?"

"The executive committee has more faith in her than you do, it seems," Nelson told him. "It's your job to keep her from signing with anyone else. Get her signature on that deal memo today, so she can't back out. And then tell her that she's going to need to move her show to New York after all. We can't compete with Letterman right down the street unless she's here."

"She's not going to go," Mitch said coldly. "You're reneging on every point that made us attractive."

"You'll have to work harder. I know you have it in you, Hayes. And what are you thinking about her for? You need to think about you. Your career. And what a coup like this is going to do for it."

"A coup like this is going to turn me into a liar and make me lose every atom of trust I've managed to build up here, Nelson." Mitch's voice deepened with conviction. "She trusts me on a personal level, and I don't know about you, but I don't have so many good friends that I can afford to alienate them."

"I just bet you're good friends," Nelson said with satisfaction. "I knew you'd take my advice and romance her. Well, playtime's over. Now it's time you justified your paycheck."

"Listen, Nelson. I want to fly back and pitch the executive committee personally, okay? There has to be a way to make them see how counterproductive this is."

"You crazy? I'm not about to authorize all that travel, even if they'd listen to you."

"At least set up a time for me to talk to them. I know you don't care one way or the other, as long as she signs. So what can it hurt?"

"It'll hurt me when they see you're wasting their time," Nelson said. "You'll be lucky to get a phone call. Don't even think about flying back here."

"All I need is fifteen minutes."

"I'll see what they say. I'm telling you, you're beating a dead horse."

And he hung up, leaving Mitch with a dead connection and a sick sense of loss around his heart.

16

EVE SHOWERED AND dressed carefully for the evening in a halter sundress that evoked the forties while emphasizing her curves in all the right places. Mitch could resign himself to enjoying the unbound look in private. When she was out in public, she had an image to maintain, and the bra that went under this dress gave her such great cleavage he'd probably be able to make do.

With a smile, she applied a touch more mascara, clipped on garnet earrings (When had Grandpa Calvert bought them for Nana? Had it been an anniversary? Their wedding?) and settled down at the dining table with the mail while she waited.

Electricity bill. Cell phone. Internet connection. Lot'O'Bucks. She ripped it open, scanned it and sighed.

Something to fax over to Jenna on Monday. That's all they needed: a ticking clock to bump up the stress another level. Here she was, in one of the most difficult periods of her life, when a woman gathered her friends around her and gained strength from their support. Jane had Perry now, so it was natural that she think of him and what he needed first, rather than her friends. Same with Nicole. Liza was so far away from them emotionally that Eve sometimes wondered if friendship was possible anymore, even if they came to some agreement about the lottery money.

She could use Liza's unconventional, no-holds-barred approach to life right now. How had it come to this? She, the relationship guru, couldn't hang on to even her oldest friendship to save her life.

Even Mitch had withdrawn emotionally—not a lot, but enough to be noticeable—when she'd brought up the subject of where they might go from here. Because of course he'd have to return to New York eventually. Would they have a long-distance affair? Doable, but not very convenient on those nights when she was feeling sexy and ready to jump him the minute he walked in the door.

Like now, for instance.

Where was he? It was nearly six—half an hour after he'd said he'd come back.

Do not call, she told herself firmly. Don't go all clingy on him. He ran into traffic, that's all. Not surprising on a Saturday evening.

The phone rang with a suddenness that made her jump. *Don't be Mitch, saying you're not coming.*

"Hi darlin', it's Grandmother."

"Hi!"

"Don't sound so surprised. Do you have a minute to chat?"

So far, Charlotte hadn't been much for chatty phone calls. Maybe this was a sign that their relationship was about to become closer. That could only be good.

"Of course. I'm just waiting for Mitch to show up.

He's late, so you can keep me from throwing ornaments at the front door while I wait."

"Mitch. He's the young man you brought to dinner?"

As if she didn't know. Eve murmured in the affirmative.

"He didn't strike me as a man who would keep you waiting long. I saw how he looked at you. Is he going to be The One?"

That surprised a chuckle out of Eve. "I have no idea, Grandmother. I sort of brought up the future earlier today and he vanished. He said he had business to do, but I think he's having a cave moment."

"Let him have it, then. He'll come around."

"I'm wearing a tangerine sundress. If that doesn't do the job, I'm taking it back."

Her grandmother laughed. Maybe this was the moment of change in a relationship that, if cordial, hadn't exactly had those moments of closeness and companionship that had marked her relationship with Nana. Although, she'd only seen Charlotte a couple of times a year, and she'd lived with Nana. Allowances had to be made. But all the same, hearing her grandmother laugh like that was almost worth the risk of revealing her hopes and fears.

If you couldn't trust your family with your inmost self, who could you trust?

Hold that thought. "I went to Mirabel today," she blurted with no lead-in whatsoever.

A careful silence hissed gently on the line. "Did you, now? And what did you think?"

"It was lovely. Smaller than I expected. Wonderful

grounds, though. Grandmother, how come we never talk about our family?"

"You obviously haven't spent enough time with Roy and Anne, honey pie."

"They talk about ancestors and people from eighty years ago. I'm talking about what it was like recently. You know, when Dad and Roy were kids."

"Did it ever occur to you that it might be painful for me to think about what was, in comparison to what is now, Eve?"

When Grandmother dropped the "honey pie," things were getting serious. Eve gave herself a mental smack. "I'm sorry. But I was talking to a docent there—it's open to the public now, part of the Ashmere Trust—and I had this moment of weirdness, knowing I was hearing more about my family from a stranger than I'd ever heard from you or Uncle Roy or even Nana Calvert."

"Who was it?"

"A lady named Adele Pierce. She said she used to babysit Dad and Uncle Roy when they were kids. Do you remember her?"

"Adele. Adele." Her grandmother sounded puzzled. "Good heavens, you don't mean Adele Crosby?"

"She said her name was Pierce. Her married name, I suppose."

"She did marry a Pierce, now that I think of it. No wonder you learned a lot…that girl was the worst gossip I ever met. She could talk the hind leg off a donkey."

"And yet, when I wanted her to talk, she wouldn't. There was a photograph there. She gave it to me. It showed Uncle Roy with his arm around Mom, and Dad standing off to the side. Did Mom date Uncle Roy before she got together with Dad?"

"When was it taken?"

"I don't know. It wasn't dated. But Mom had hair down to her waist, parted in the middle. And platform shoes. So I'd guess early seventies. She couldn't have been more than sixteen."

"I have no memory of such a picture, or why it would be at Mirabel instead of in one of our photo albums."

"Uncle Roy donated copies of some pictures to the trust. Adele gave me the original, though. Maybe it got mixed in by mistake."

"Maybe. Your mother was good friends with both my boys, Eve. They hung around together like the Three Musketeers, until Gibson and then Roy went off to college."

Her tone was dismissive, as though the picture were insignificant. Maybe it was. But there was something in the expression of that boy who had become her dad—some hurt, some pain that the camera had caught—that made her reluctant to let it go. And there had been that swift change of subject on Adele's part, too.

"Honey pie, the girls are at the door for our book club meeting. I need to go."

"Bye, Grandmother. I'll call you next week."

"You do that. I want to hear more about your young man."

Eve hung up with a smile, and went to get her notebook out of her handbag. Still no sign of Mitch, and it was ten past six. There must have been an accident on the freeway. Well, if he wasn't here by six-thirty, she'd call the restaurant and move their reservation out another half hour.

Adele Crosby Pierce answered her phone on the fourth ring, about when Eve expected it to jump to voice mail.

"Oh, hello, dear. How nice of you to call."

She didn't seem bothered that Eve had tracked down her phone number. But then, her mind lived in a different era, when people called to get a recipe, not to steal a person's identity or stalk them.

"I wanted to thank you again for showing us around Mirabel, and for giving me this picture of my family," she began.

"You're most welcome. I love to introduce people to the past, you know. And today it was particularly lovely, since it was *your* past."

Nothing like plunging right in. Eve took a fortifying breath. "That's what I wanted to ask you about, Adele. This picture that you gave me. Is there some kind of story behind it?"

Silence.

Eve went on, "It seemed to startle you when I asked questions about it, so I wondered if perhaps you would rather talk about it in private. That's the reason for my call."

"That's very considerate of you, dear. You're the second person who's asked about it."

"Oh? Who was the other?" Uncle Roy? Mitch?

"I didn't catch his name. He said he worked for your television station, though. A terribly nice young man."

She must be referring to Dylan's call, earlier, and

gotten it muddled up. "Anyway, I was wondering if you'd tell me about the picture, that's all."

Another pause. "You know I abhor gossip of any kind, dear."

Eve thought about what Grandmother would think of this, and smothered a smile. "So do I. Though giving me your memories of my family isn't gossip, is it?"

"No, I suppose not. Yet, I don't want to hurt anyone. It wasn't dear Charlotte's fault that Loreen couldn't talk to her. Or Isabel's either, for that matter. But I was so close to those boys, and even in those days, they would have sent her away anyway."

"Sent who away?"

"Loreen, of course. But I'm not going to say any more. It isn't my place. You take that picture over to your Uncle Roy and ask him to explain."

"Uncle Roy?"

"I'll bet you fifty dollars that picture got put in the donation pile on purpose. So it was out of the house. You go ask him."

"But—"

"I'm no gossip. A man should clean up his own messes, in my opinion, and this one's been a mess for nearly thirty years."

With that, she hung up.

Eve stared at the receiver in her hand, utterly mystified. "It's a *picture,*" she said to it, and hung it up. When she did so, it beeped, signifying that a call had come in while she'd been talking. She pressed the playback button.

"Eve, it's Mitch." He sounded agitated. She'd been

right, then. He'd probably driven past a wreck on the freeway. "I'm sorry, but I have to cancel our plans tonight. Something's come up with the deal, and it's important I figure out the best way to fight this fire. I'm looking at flights to New York right now. I'll fly up there on my own dime if I have to. I don't know if…whether you…" A sigh of frustration. "I feel like shit. I'll do my best to straighten this out. Goodbye."

The answering machine winked off, leaving Eve sitting in her best tangerine dress with no evening, no answers and most important…no Mitch.

Eve Best, you're not going to take this sitting down.

Within sixty seconds, she'd grabbed her bag and car keys and was backing the car out of the driveway. If he booked a flight online, she had maybe twenty minutes while he scrolled through his options. Add ten to that if he checked out of the hotel. If the traffic gods smiled on her, she could get to the Ritz before he walked out.

The time for sitting around and waiting was long gone, if it had ever existed. She'd already decided that she was tired of living a life on the surface, endlessly talking about things that mattered instead of actually taking a risk and experiencing them.

Well, she was going to take a risk now. If Mitch got on that plane, something deep inside told her he wouldn't come back. Okay, so he hadn't responded quite the way she'd expected him to when she'd brought up a future together. She could handle that. Hadn't she done a whole show on the caveman mystique? She and the girls had even turned it into a catchphrase: the "cave moment." That crucial juncture in a relationship when

a guy pulled away and went into his cave to think or
flee or whatever they did when they faced the naked
truth of a woman's feelings. Sometimes he never came
out. And sometimes he had to be coaxed out with the
warmth of a good fire.

Eve had plenty of fire, and she wasn't about to let
Mitch fly out of her life without getting one more taste of
it.

Twenty-three minutes later, she pulled up to the front
doors and leaped out.

"Hey, aren't you Eve Best?" The valet looked about
twenty, so Eve pulled out all the stops in the smile she
turned on him.

"How sweet of you to recognize me," she said. "Would
you mind looking after my car for just a moment?"

"No, ma'am," he said, blinking at the sheer wattage
of the smile, and she tossed him the car keys and a tip.

"Thank you, sugar." God, she was turning into her
grandmother. But hey, whatever worked.

Two steps inside the lobby, she realized the hotel was
hosting some kind of computer electronics convention.
Crowds of men wearing everything from iPods to Ralph
Lauren milled on the carpet. She wove between them,
heading for the front desk—and arrived in time to see
Mitch turn away, tucking his credit card into his wallet
and picking up the handle of his rolling suitcase.

"Mitch!"

He blinked as she rushed up to him. "How did you
get here?"

"Drove. Fast. Tell me you didn't check out."

He glanced over his shoulder at the mob pressing

itself toward the harried clerks behind the counter. "I have a ten o'clock flight to LaGuardia. Just as well. This place is a madhouse."

"Ask them to reinstate you."

"Are you kidding? My room's probably already gone."

She thought fast. "Then come home with me."

His face looked tired—not quite defeated, but getting there—and her heart squeezed. "I can't, Eve." She took his arm and guided him toward the door. He didn't seem to notice. "My boss talked to the executive committee and they want to change the terms of the deal. Apparently they want you to be the next Letterman."

"Letterman doesn't do daytime." She smiled her thanks to the valet and Mitch, who obviously thought she was taking him to the airport, got into her car. She'd let him think that. For now.

"I know. They want you to move to New York, and they'll create a late-night show for you."

Sliding behind the wheel, she said, "We already agreed I'm staying here."

"Yes, but the deal memo isn't signed yet. My instructions are to get you to agree to the new terms, or else. So I'm going to New York to meet with them personally. It's a long shot, but I have to convince them they're shooting themselves and the network in the foot."

"You don't need to go all that way." She sped up the on-ramp to the freeway.

"I feel I do. Nelson said he'd set up a phone call, but that won't cut it. I have to do this in person to have any chance of convincing them."

One exit. Two. The next one was hers.

"It's a helluva trip, though." He rubbed the back of his neck, as if stress were making his muscles seize up. "There aren't any nonstops at this time of night, so I have to route through North Carolina and Philly. I get in at some ungodly hour in the morning, but I had to take what I could get. I just hope I'm coherent."

The things he was willing to do in order to keep his word—or at least the network's word. Talk about above and beyond. That meant something, didn't it? Surely he couldn't be motivated strictly by loyalty to the network? There had to be more to it than that.

"I have a better idea."

"You do? Hey!" He sat up as she took her exit. "This isn't the way to the airport. Do you want me to miss my flight?"

"You don't need to kill yourself doing this, Mitch," she told him. "You don't need to fly to New York when we have a network feed right at the station. What's the point of technology if not to use it?"

He stared at her, and then his gaze narrowed, as if he was remembering something. "You have a video linkup. I saw it the first day I was there."

"Right. We can beam your pitch right to CWB's head office. And I happen to know a damn good executive producer who could run, say, a kick-butt presentation with a voice-over and graphics if you wanted. We're all in this together, right?"

She pulled into her driveway and shut the engine off. He was looking at her as though she had just announced the cure for cancer.

"I knew there was a reason I was crazy about you," he said.

She grinned. Maybe her tangerine sundress wasn't going to be wasted tonight. After all, it was the color of fire.

17

"YOU'RE RIGHT. It was a total cave moment. All men have them and all women have to learn to deal with them."

Jane brushed the excess powder off Eve's nose and turned her face toward the light with the gentle fingers of long friendship.

"I agree." Nicole, with her ever-present clipboard in her lap, pulled her legs up under her and watched the two of them in the dressing-room mirror. "When a woman tells a guy she thinks it's more than a fling, his first instinct is to run."

"But last night…" Eve's voice trailed off, and she caught Jane and Nicole exchanging an amused look. The station's dressing room had become the equivalent of a girls' clubhouse, and she'd just told them everything. Except about the puzzling photograph. That was private—and she wasn't sure she wanted to dig any more, anyway. Grandmother thought it was nothing, so it probably was. She had bigger fish to fry.

"Can I just say that the man is fabulous in bed and funny to boot? What sane woman wouldn't want to keep him around, and tell him so? I took a risk. I was honest. Now it's up to him. Unless he thinks making love is the answer."

Jane examined her work with a critical eye. "Eve, not everyone is as forthright as you about their relationships. And it does look kind of bad that he tried to leave town practically as soon as your agreement about the show was in his hand."

So Jane had heard the rumors, too. "Mitchell Hayes did not romance me to get the show. He really does care about whether I'm happy." He'd been prepared to fly all night for her. The least she could do was show some faith—unlike some people. "I'm not a teenager. I can tell when a man is sincere. And he is." The pain she'd seen in his face was proof of that. Wasn't it? "He couldn't have made love to me the way he did last night if his feelings weren't real. We all know that some men communicate through action. For them, it's not about the words."

"Eve, Eve," Nicole said, shaking her head. "You did a show about this only last week. 'Is What He Says Really What He Means?' Maybe you should do one called 'It's in His Kiss,' like that song."

"I think that stripper housewife said it all," Jane put in. "'All that's real during sex is sex. Anything else is gravy.'"

"Ow." Eve winced. "Easy on the hair."

"Don't jerk back like that, then." Jane loosened her grip on the curling iron. "We don't want you expecting gravy when all there is is meat. No pun intended."

"Ha. And here I thought you guys would help me build up the nerve to try to talk with him about it again."

"I'll be happier when he comes out of his cave and tells you something honest, with real words," Jane said. "Until then, I'm reserving judgment."

"We still need to address this rumor that you two are an item," Nicole added. "Even if you are, we still have to maintain your privacy. The answering service has had half a dozen calls from that rag-mag *Peachtree Free Press,* over the last twenty-four hours. Every one of them was for you. I don't know how they got wind of who you're dating."

"The tabs can screw themselves."

"They usually do, with the crap they print," Nicole said. "The *Free Press* is one of the worst, though I must say their cameraman must love you. Your pictures are always great."

"I never talk to the tabs, and they know it. Okay, Jane. Am I ready?"

"Ready and able. You've got half an hour to prep, so make the most of it. And here's your bug."

Eve took the wireless transmitter and fitted it in her ear. Because she had a habit of rambling around before the show in an effort to control her adrenaline, Cole had invested in the bug so he could give her the countdown without tying her to her desk. With a final tug at the hem of a new beaded tank, Eve strode down the hall toward the set, where the guys in the control booth would be doing sound and lighting checks before showtime at three.

But underneath it all the question of Mitch nagged and prodded at her. Was she wrong to want resolution? Why wouldn't he talk about them, even when he was wrapped in her arms, with no one to listen in but the night? Communicating through action seemed to be a male thing. Maybe she needed to do that. But how?

Through the thin false walls of the studio, the noise levels rose as the doors opened and the audience began to file in. Her thoughts spun on as her blood began to pump in anticipation. Deciding to act—to take a risk and reach out for what she wanted—was one thing.

But finding the courage to do it was quite another. Because what if, after she tried again, he got on that plane anyway and left her?

THE EXECUTIVE COMMITTEE at CWB had agreed to the video link at three-thirty, which worked out perfectly. Eve would still be on the set, mingling with her audience, and she wouldn't be able to watch his attempt to turn this fiasco around. Mitch would rather have no witnesses, thanks. What he did want was to succeed. To come out with a gift safe in his hand—her show, intact, exactly the way she wanted it.

He glanced at his watch. He had an hour yet. Cole Crawford had given him a brief window of time to put some bells and whistles on the presentation he'd been working on all morning. But Mitch had it all in his head. He'd been living this for weeks, after all.

He was still amazed that Nelson Berg had gotten out of his way and agreed to this. Mitch was the one who had the information at his fingertips. He knew the talent. But primarily, he was the most heavily invested in winning.

With everything up in the air—his job, the show, his

future—the only thing he had left to hang on to was Eve's simple admission of her feelings. As far as he was concerned, that was worth taking a chance on. That was worth figuring out the logistics of time and distance for. He could probably hub out of Atlanta for most of his trips instead of Chicago or Dallas, so he'd be able to see her once or twice a week. Lots of relationships survived on less than that.

"Mr. Hayes!"

Mitch blinked and raised his head. Dylan Moore stood in the doorway, panting.

"I've been searching the station for you. Come on—it's showtime."

Puzzled, he got up. "I'm not going to be in the audience for *Just Between Us*. I'm doing a video link in the newsroom."

Dylan made a rolling movement with his hand. "I know, I know. It's started and there's a panel of suits waiting for you."

"But it's only two-thirty. I've got an hour yet."

Dylan shook his head. "Not according to them, Mr. Hayes. I don't know what time zone they're in, but it's not eastern."

"Shit!"

He took the stairs three at a time and skidded into the small studio, which held not much more than a couple of lights, a stationary camera and a desk behind which someone could transmit breaking news or a timely interview. A technician nodded at him and pointed at a monitor, where—thank you, God—Cole Crawford had loaded his presentation.

He only hoped he hadn't left his carefully thought-out arguments back there at the top of the stairs.

He knew most of the network's execs by sight. Three men and two women. As he slid into the chair and Nelson introduced him—without editorial comments on his tardiness—he made careful note of each name and position, so he could target his appeal personally. His aptitude for memorizing music came in handy in these kinds of applications.

And then he went to work.

With the right amount of detail, he explained to the people on the big flat-panel screen why *Just Between Us* worked so well in the regional market. Looking steadily into the camera, he outlined the team approach, and the talents of each of Eve's production people that gave the show its own distinct flavor.

"Remember what happened with *The X-Files* when it went to Los Angeles?" he said. "The Vancouver production team had created that unique atmosphere and mood that was almost a third character in the show. When it moved, a vital element seeped away and it changed. And, I might point out, it only lasted a couple more seasons. We don't want that to happen to *Just Between Us.*"

The execs looked at each other, and the woman on the left nodded. The others shrugged, and Mitch tapped the keyboard in front of him to move on to the financial projections. As he might have expected, the numbers got more attention than a discussion of production values, but that was okay.

A move to New York was wrong on so many levels

that every point he could make only added to the solidity of his case.

At last, he wound up with, "You should know that CBS and SBN have made very lucrative offers to Eve and her team, and she turned them down in favor of CWB simply because the others wanted her to move to New York. Please reconsider this move, ladies and gentlemen. It would not be in the best interests of the show, its personnel, the network...or our viewers."

With that, he sat back and prepared himself to field the inevitable barrage of difficult questions. But to his surprise, Nelson Berg stepped into view as the execs began to pack up their notepads and laptops.

"Thanks, Mitch. You've been very helpful in laying out the case. Don't terminate the connection, please. I want to have a word, since I've got you here."

Mitch took some deep breaths while he watched five people file out of camera range and waited for the adrenaline to stop zooming through his system.

Off camera, Mitch heard a door close, and Nelson seated himself at the table, smack in the middle of the screen. The guy was impossible to read on the best of days—that face was usually set in a frown of disapproval. Mitch resisted the urge to ask—beg—for information.

Nelson sighed and steepled his fingers over his stomach. "You made a good pitch."

"Thanks."

"I couldn't have done better myself. The video link was a good idea. Nice cost-saving measure. Shows you're a team player. Unfortunately, it didn't change their minds."

What? How could it not?

"It's insane to bring that show to New York and you know it." Mitch felt hope draining out of him with every word. "Is there anything I can do that will convince them?"

"Afraid not. They were shaking their heads before they even left the studio."

"I could run the numbers again. Do some more research."

"It won't do any good. It's unanimous, Mitch. Stop beating your head against the wall."

"This is going to kill them."

"Who? The people there?"

"Yes. They won't come. I can guarantee you'll lose this deal if you make me walk down that hall and tell them this."

"I can guarantee you'll lose your job if you don't." The words, as usual, were brutal. Like being hammered over the head. But Nelson's expression was less sour than usual. "I'm sorry, Mitch, but sometimes we have to take it on the chin. You were a big success at getting Eve to commit the show to CWB against the odds. You can do it again. I have faith in you."

Eve had faith in him, too. Cold despair touched his heart as he thought of those long talks in the park, when he'd come to understand that a simple conversation about the workings of this business was nearly impossible for a woman like her. How happy he'd been to fill that need—and all her other needs, too. He thought of Eve, head thrown back on her pillow as she groaned in ecstasy under him just last night, opening up to him utterly, making herself vulnerable for the sake of the pleasure they made together.

How could he find her and tell her that all the plans they'd agreed to would be snatched out from under her? Would she ever trust the network again?

To hell with that. Would she ever trust *him* again?

"I can't do it, Nelson." The words came out of his mouth before he could bite them back.

"It's a dirty job, but it's *your* job." He leaned forward, his gaze stony. "You and I don't make these decisions, Mitch. We just make 'em happen."

"Well, this one isn't going to happen. Not with me."

"Is that a threat?" Nelson sounded amazed. It wasn't Nelson's fault—he was simply the messenger. Mitch couldn't remember the last time he'd stood up to what the network's management wanted. Maybe he never had. Maybe that's why he was so damned unhappy with his job. And why he didn't have a life.

"Of course not," he said. "I'm offering you my resignation."

Nelson's jaw—well, it didn't drop, but its usual grim clamp got looser. "You're overreacting. Pull it together, Hayes. We have work to do."

"No, Nelson. What we have here is a lose-lose situation. You told me before that if I didn't complete this acquisition, you'd be forced to give me my walking papers. If you send me out of here with these terms, I'll lose the deal. So whether I resign now or you fire me tomorrow, I'm still out of a job." It wouldn't take long to compose a resignation letter and send it. "I prefer to leave on my own terms. I'll have an official letter on your desk in half an hour, and I'll take the two weeks' vacation I have coming in lieu of notice."

"You're making a mistake," Nelson warned. "You can't leave this deal half-baked. Who's going to go down there and finish it?"

Mitch looked into the camera, knowing his face must look as grave as Nelson's did on the screen. "Someone who doesn't give a rat's ass about Eve and her people, that's who."

_18_

EVE COULDN'T HAVE moved out of the studio doorway if the building had been burning down.

She watched as Mitch closed his laptop and put it in his briefcase. He nodded his thanks to the technician in the control booth, and the video screen went dark.

And then he turned toward the door and saw her.

Their gazes collided, and it seemed to Eve that a silent explosion happened right there in the middle of the room. How could she bear the pain in that gaze? And how could she put into words this maelstrom of emotion whirling inside her as she realized what he'd just done?

He'd thrown away his career for her.

The enormity of it staggered her. Humbled her. And showed her the depth of her own feelings for him. Instead of reaching out hesitantly, throwing out hints and signals the way she'd been doing, he'd gambled his whole future in one grand act for her sake. Could she really have underestimated him that much? How blind could she be?

"How long have you been standing there?"

Eve leaned on the door and the On Air light went out as the technician exited the back of the booth and moved on to his next task. They were alone—and the studio was soundproof.

"A few minutes. I slipped in when you were running the financials."

"So you heard Nelson Berg."

"And I heard you. Oh, Mitch, you don't have to do this." Her voice trembled, and she swallowed.

"What else could I have done? They had me between a rock and a hard place. Either way, I would lose— because I know damn well you aren't going to New York. Or am I wrong?"

Why was he still standing there behind the desk? Why wasn't he pulling her into his arms? "No, you aren't wrong. In fact, you're amazingly right." Maybe he only had one grand gesture in him. Maybe it was up to her to take this the rest of the way. Eve gathered her courage and circled the desk.

"Right for the show, and right for me," she said softly. "When I heard you say that, I—"

"Eve, ten minutes," Cole said in her ear. "Guest's in the green room waiting for you."

Ten minutes that could change her life.

She reached out to lay a hand on Mitch's sleeve, but he picked up his briefcase instead. "Mitch, don't go. I want to talk to you, but I just got my ten-minute call."

"I'm unemployed. I have all the time in the world."

His voice was hollow. What did he expect from her? She had to say something, quick.

"I appreciate that you'd do such a thing for my sake. I know what it must have cost you. And I want you to know that it—it just makes me love you all the more."

"What?"

"I mean it. But I've got to go. Please don't leave. Meet me in my office after the show. Promise."

What did that look in his eyes mean? Pain, wonder, confusion. Oh God, why did this have to happen seven minutes before showtime? Why did he look like that?

If it were up to her, she'd stay right here in this studio and show him exactly what she meant—preferably horizontally on the news desk. But the two hundred and fifty people in Studio One would probably stage a riot.

Briefcase nothwithstanding, she grabbed him by his lapels and planted a kiss on his mouth as full of promise as she could make it. "In my office," she repeated, and ran.

With no time to process what had just happened, she thought she'd make a complete hash of the show, but instead, she found herself drawn right into the topic: the chemistry of love. Nicole had produced a researcher from the local university, and the man was only too happy to explain his life's work to her. And in view of the last half hour, it was illuminating.

"It's a well-known fact that job loss is one of the greatest contributors to male depression," the guy said. "But what we've discovered is that rejection—which is what losing a job really is, right?—causes the production of testosterone in a man's body to drop. That's what leads to depression, withdrawal and loss of self-esteem."

"So what can he do to come out of it?" Eve leaned in to ask. Was this a sign from heaven, or what? Bless Nicole. She was getting a raise for this.

"Well, he can go down to the gym and shoot some

baskets," the researcher said, "or he can make love to his wife."

"Hear that, ladies?" Eve asked the audience. "If any of you have unemployed partners out there, your duty to his testosterone is clear."

The audience cracked up, and she finished with her monologue, feeling as though a lightbulb had gone off in her head. She couldn't do anything about Mitch's decision to end it with CWB, but by God, she could help him through what had to be the most stressful afternoon of his life.

Boy, could she help. He'd already said he had plans for her desk, hadn't he?

She sprinted up the stairs and arrived in her office breathing fast with anticipation. Would he be there? He had to be. He couldn't have gone off to his cave at a moment like this, not when she had the cure for what ailed him—

"Eve?"

He turned from the window when she burst in. "Oh, thank God. I was convinced you'd be on that plane."

"I should be. I need to start networking. Putting out feelers. Talking to people. You know the drill."

He sounded so distant. But she wouldn't let him get away with it. *Not with your testosterone levels circling the drain. Have I got a cure for you. The marvels of modern—and very ancient—chemistry.*

"I have a better idea." She wrapped her arms around him and pressed up against his back. "Seems to me you made some rash promises about my desk. Want me to lock the door?"

He chuckled and turned, and his arms went around her. This was more like it. "Believe me when I say I'd like nothing better—if I can take a rain check. You understand, don't you? I'm shell-shocked right now. My brain is zooming at top speed—only it's going in circles."

"Mine is, too," she said against the soft wool of his suit jacket. "But you're in the middle. I meant what I said down there in the studio, Mitch. About—" *Do it. Dive right in, like he did.* "—about loving you. I want to make sure that, at least, is clear between us."

He drew back to look into her eyes. "How can you love an unemployed failure? A woman like you—beautiful, the one everyone wants? The self-made woman who pulled herself up from tragedy to be a celebrity? Trust me, Eve, you have a whole world of choices out there. You don't need to settle for what's at hand."

Loss of self-esteem. She was going to have to invite that researcher back. The man was a gold mine.

"You've been reading too many headlines. A woman would be crazy *not* to grab a guy who would sacrifice himself and his career to protect her happiness. And believe me, I ain't crazy."

Gently, he set her away from him, and a chill prickled over her skin. *Withdrawal.*

"I need some time alone. We both do. I think it would be best if—"

A muffled sound from behind her closed office door made them both turn. "No! I absolutely forbid it," Dylan said outside.

"She's got to know," a female voice said. "Better I

tell her than she gets blindsided in the hall or worse, during town hall tomorrow."

"Girl, you ain't goin' in there and showin' her that. What kind of a friend are you?"

Whatever it was must be serious if it made Dylan revert to what he called "informal speech."

"Dylan?" Eve called. "What's going on?"

"Nothing." A torrent of hissed whispering ensued, and something thumped against the wood.

Eve crossed the room and jerked the door open. Nicole practically fell into her office, Dylan right behind. Each of them hung onto a side of a rag-mag that Eve recognized as the *Peachtree Free Press*.

Nicole gave a final yank and ripped the tabloid out of Dylan's hands. Flushed with triumph, she glared at him, then turned to Eve.

"*Some people* might think it's better to keep you in the dark, but I thought you'd want to see this," she said.

"What?" Eve took the paper.

And then everything seemed to fall away as time ground to a halt.

TV MILLIONAIRE'S SECRET REVEALED
EVE BEST IS TYCOON'S DAUGHTER

Eve Best, the darling of daytime talk shows, Atlanta's go-to girl for everything the city wants to know about sex and relationships, has been hiding a relationship of her own. No, not the handsome executive arm candy from CWB recently seen squiring her about town. This relationship goes deeper into the dark secrets of her past.

A recent investigation has revealed that Eve, supposed daughter of the late Gibson Best, who died tragically in a car accident in 1990, is not Gibson's daughter at all. Rather, she is the illegitimate child of tycoon Roy Best, Gibson's brother, who married socialite and Atlanta Ballet Theatre director Anne Delancey in 1985.

A close family friend, who declined to be named, has known the ugly truth for years and only recently was prevailed on to bring it to light. "I'm no gossip, mind," says the source, "but those boys confided in me right up until they went away to college. I've kept my mouth closed for nearly thirty years, but that poor girl deserves to know that her father did not die in that crash. Her real father, that is."

All Atlanta knows that, as a member of the old-money set, Best used her social connections and obligations to pull some golden strings, propelling her from the obscure position of junior weathergirl to that of Atlanta's most popular TV star. But how far will she go now that it's known she's not entitled to the Best name in quite the way she thought?

According to our source, Loreen Calvert Best became pregnant by Roy Best just before he went away to Yale. Gibson went to school, too, but before he left, he married the deserted Loreen in a secret ceremony attended only by our source as witness. When Roy came home, he went into business, trading on the Best name to attain a fortune in the electronics and then the real estate markets. He married Anne Delancey in what was then billed as the Wedding of the Year, and two other children followed immediately.

Repeated calls to Eve Best at CATL-TV have gone unanswered. Roy Best has refused comment.

The investigative staff at *Peachtree Free Press* challenge Eve Best to come out of hiding and tell her viewers the real story. After all, why should she put the blinding spotlight on the secrets of others on live television when she's so unwilling to bring her own to the light of day?

Eve looked up, and Dylan flinched. She could only imagine what her face must look like. Nicole reached out a tentative hand and laid it on Eve's shoulder. "Are you okay?"

"I'm fine."

"No, you're not. Nobody could be fine after reading something like this."

Mitch took the paper from her and scanned the article. "It's a bucket of lies, Eve. They're just trying to sell more of their lousy rag."

"You've never heard this rumor before?" Nicole asked.

"Never." But the word rang hollow. Because it would explain that photo. And Adele Pierce—so obviously the paper's so-called source—who had said Uncle Roy needed to clean up his mess. And Aunt Anne at dinner, behaving so strangely. What had she said? Something about the truth.

"I have to talk to my uncle," Eve blurted. "Today. This minute."

"You're not driving anywhere after a shock like this." Mitch picked her cropped linen jacket off the back of her chair and handed it to her. "I'll take you."

Her phone rang, and Dylan picked it up, waving the two of them toward the door. Then he called, "Eve. There's a visitor in the lobby for you."

"Not interested. We'll go out the back door."

"Yeah, you are. It's your uncle."

Eve stopped dead in the middle of the carpet. "My Uncle Roy? Is downstairs? Now?"

Dylan nodded.

She resisted the urge to ask Dylan why he wasn't already on his way to fetch him. "Escort him in here, please, Dylan. And find us some brandy or something. Don't look at me like that—this is a crisis. Raid Dan's office—I know he's got liquor in his sideboard."

Mitch backed toward the door. "I'll give the two of you some privacy. This is a family matter."

She grabbed his jacket. "Please don't. I need you. Please."

For a moment, she thought she'd lose him—that the shaken self-confidence he'd allowed to swamp him earlier would come back and separate them just when she needed him more than ever before. But then a new expression filled his eyes, and he straightened his shoulders.

"You do?"

"Yes." She burrowed into his arms and felt like shouting hallelujah as they went around her body, strong and sure. "Now. Later. Forever. Just stay."

And that's how her Uncle Roy found them when Dylan ushered him in a moment later. Dylan put a brand-new bottle of Courvoisier and three ceramic coffee mugs from the kitchen on her low table and shut the door behind him.

Roy Best looked as though he didn't know what to do with himself. He stood uneasily, searching Eve's face, no doubt for some clue as to her feelings.

She could have helped him out if she'd only known herself what those were. To give herself a moment to find her equilibrium, Eve poured a shot for all of them, then sat next to her uncle on the short couch. Roy was neatly put together in an expensive suit and sober tie, but his face…he looked as though he were in shock.

Maybe he was. Even though Mitch stood behind her, Roy didn't seem to be aware there was anyone but Eve in the room.

"You must hate me," he said at last, swirling the brandy in the mug but not sipping it. She supposed they were committing some kind of brandy sin by not drinking it out of snifters, but they had to work with what they were given.

"Of course not," she assured him softly. "I only saw the paper just now, but ever since I went to Mirabel on the weekend, I've seen and heard things that have puzzled me. The paper has one slant that would explain them. I'd love to hear yours, if you want to tell me."

He gave up on the drink and put it on the table. "That's just it. It isn't slanted. Except for the nasty tone of it, the paper has its essentials correct. I'm your biological father."

Luke, I am your father, she heard James Earl Jones say in her head. *You look like Evalyne,* Adele said, her voice threading over it. *So does my niece. She's fourteen,* her own voice said, adding to the mix. She wasn't blond, like both Loreen and her da—Gibson. She was a green-eyed brunette. Like Evalyne. Like Roy.

"Do Karen and Emily know?" she rasped, her throat dry. "And Aunt Anne?" She took a gulp of the brandy, and it burned all the way down.

"Anne has always known. Do you think I would keep something like that from her? When you were eleven, and fixing to come out here for Christmas a few weeks before the accident, she wanted us to tell you then. Your mom agreed, but your dad was dead against it."

"They had a fight in the car," Eve said, remembering. "They went out somewhere, and even before they left, they were fighting. That was the night they went off the road. Because they were fighting about me." Her voice dropped as she spiraled down the tunnel of time to a place she thought she'd blocked out. The flashing lights outside the house. Nana running to stop the policeman on the sidewalk. The funeral, with two closed caskets that she to this day had a difficult time believing contained her parents' bodies. They'd never let her see them. It wasn't fitting, Nana had insisted.

Maybe not, but she'd never been able to say goodbye, either. Hadn't been able to control the situation. Hadn't been able to give vent to the depths of emotion she'd been feeling. Going deep into emotion hurt too much. She couldn't bear it then.

Things have changed now, haven't they? Because of Mitch.

"We can't know that," Roy said heavily. "Believe me, I've had my share of regrets over this. But it seemed kinder to let things go on as they were. The kids think of you as their cousin, not their half sister. That will change now, of course. And I'll be asking their forgiveness, too."

"I have close family." She marveled that she was only now realizing it. "If you want to acknowledge that."

His face crumpled. "Acknowledge? I'm begging your forgiveness, Eve. For being such a coward. For letting Gibson clean up my mistake. For what it's worth, he adored your mother, even while Loreen and I were dating. I think he would have done what he did a hundred times rather than let her face those uptight society biddies who would have looked down their noses at her."

"She loved him, too," Eve said softly. "It was the right thing to do, their getting married. I had a great childhood. And maybe it prepared me for what I do for a living now."

"I'm glad to hear it. Anne will be glad, too. She's been absolutely beside herself, hardly knowing whether to blame me or comfort me. Adele called, you know. That's why I got here so early. I don't read that particular paper, so when she told me what that reporter had written, I broke a couple of speed limits getting over here."

"I have a few things I'd like to say to that woman," Eve said grimly.

"Don't be too hard on her. She was absolutely right. She's been nagging me for thirty years, just the way she used to nag us to brush our teeth and quit talking after she turned out the lights."

"It was none of her business."

"Maybe not, but you'd have a hard time telling her that. It's the way families are around here. My mom—your grandmother—had to go out to work, you know. She couldn't be home much for us, so Adele stepped in to help. She became a kind of second mother. A confidante, in many ways. Even for Loreen."

"I'm sure Grandmother did what she had to, to keep body and soul together." She couldn't blame a woman for that.

He nodded. "That's in the past. I'm most concerned about the present. Are you going to be all right?"

Unexpectedly, her throat closed up, and she nodded. "I think so. This is a lot to take in." She glanced at him through her lashes. "It might be a while before I can call you Dad instead of Uncle Roy."

Tears trembled at the corners of his eyes. "I'll do my best to earn that honor," he said gruffly.

And then he pulled her into his arms.

19

MITCH LEANED BACK in his chair—Row 1, Seat 8, reserved for special guests—and studied the raucous crowd around him in the studio as they waited for "All About Eve" to begin. With the story of her parentage out, the wires were burning up and the media were having a field day. There had even been an invitation this morning to appear on Letterman on Monday night—no doubt a last-ditch effort by Chad Everard to convince her to come over to the dark side. Mitch had the feeling it might backfire, though, and do nothing but give *Just Between Us* a nice boost in the ratings.

He also hoped she'd accept, so he could go with her and show her the sights of New York before he called a Realtor and put his condo up for sale.

Because he'd discovered that mundane things like nailing down a job worked a lot differently here in the South. Armed with nothing but a phone number and Eve's belief in him, he'd decided to face reality head-on, knowing that to get what you wanted out of life, you had to get out there and ask for it. The way she had. And while Eve was doing her prep work this morning, he'd gone for the most unusual job interview he'd ever had.

When she wrapped today's show, they were definitely going to celebrate. And maybe he'd even come through on his promise and make use of her desk. So far, today was turning into a very good day to try things for the first time.

Applause broke out all around him, and there she was. She took her seat alone at the front of the stage, a single spotlight beaming down on her.

God, she looked good. His heart turned over.

"Good afternoon, Atlanta," she said. "I'm Eve Best, and I'd like to keep this just between us."

The audience roared, and she made jokes with the people in the front row until the noise died down. Then she looked directly into the camera, which was positioned above the audience so that she looked directly at them, too. Mitch sat mesmerized by the emotion in her wide green eyes.

"Today I'd like to do something different with our town-hall meeting. Y'all know what I want to talk about. My family. You guys have been with me through thick and thin. If anyone is going to get me through this, it's my friends, and I count y'all among them."

Shouts of approval and another burst of applause.

"So, that said, lemme have it, Atlanta. What do you want to know about what you've been reading in the papers and seeing on TV?"

Two production assistants roamed the audience with wireless microphones, picking people at random. The camera zoomed in on the first volunteer, a heavyset woman with apple-red cheeks.

"First of all, Eve," she said, her voice trembling with

nervousness, "is it really true or a bunch of made-up gossip aimed at selling papers?"

Over the laughter, Eve said, "It's true. My biological father is Roy Best. He and my mother dated before he went away to college. He was young, only eighteen, and when you're eighteen, maybe you don't make the kinds of decisions that last well over a lifetime. He chose to leave when my mother told him she was pregnant."

"Bastard!" someone yelled.

"Not to my knowledge," Eve said calmly. "But you can ask my grandmother. She's sitting right over here."

The camera zoomed in on Charlotte Best, who was sitting a few seats down from Mitch and whose cheekbones were a force to be reckoned with. Mitch grinned as she quartered the studio, located the guy who'd yelled and pinned him with a glare.

"Sorry, ma'am," the guy said, subsiding into his seat.

"But meanwhile," Eve went on, "the man I'll always think of as *Dad* had been carrying a torch for my mom for years. Since grade school, I think. Anyway, she married him instead and gave me the happiest childhood a kid could ask for. Except for the accident that took them away from me, I wouldn't change a thing."

You go, love. Mitch's heart swelled with emotion at her bravery. He knew what it had taken for her to choose dealing with this head-on instead of hiding behind her legal team and maintaining the chilly, private silence that Charlotte would have preferred. That would only have inflamed the media into a frenzy. This way, she controlled people's impression of her, and the media would have to take her leftovers.

She was brave. She was brilliant.

She was the best thing that had ever happened to him.

The PA handed the microphone to a middle-aged woman with a couple of kids sitting on either side. "Have you been able to forgive your uncle for what he did to your mom?"

Ouch. Mitch winced for Eve's sake, but her expression only softened.

"The same afternoon the story came out, my father came to my office to tell me everything. Now I feel I know him better than ever—and I love him more than ever, too. It takes a brave man to admit he made a mistake." She paused. "The mistake I mean was that he didn't tell me years ago. As for him leaving my mom, I don't see that as a mistake. Not now. Not when it turned out that Gibson and Loreen were actually right for one another."

They cut to commercial then, and Mitch dragged in a deep breath. Funny how he'd been so tense, as though he'd been afraid her audience would draw and quarter her over what could have been a scandal.

But she was carrying it off so well. She knew her viewers. The reason they tuned in was because she was honest, spontaneous and had the kind of positive energy that you'd want in a best friend. That's what she was doing. Treating her viewers like her friends. Maybe that resulted in the necessity for a few restraining orders, but on the whole its biggest result was a devoted following who tuned in day after day.

CWB had been insane to think of taking her out of this environment. To disregard the slow-growth plan.

Mitch had no doubt they'd come to regret it, especially if Eve wound up with another network.

The monitors flickered and they were back. Mitch focused on Eve with as much attention as Zach, who was up there behind him operating the crane.

This time, a guy in his twenties had the microphone. "So, is it true that you've been offered a spot on a national network if you, like, move to L.A.?"

"It's true," Eve said. "And it's New York, not L.A. I'm not going." She spread her hands as the audience erupted with cheers. "How could I go without taking y'all with me?"

Laughter. Mitch saw that the guy hadn't relinquished the mike. "So that exec guy you were dating, is he out of the picture? Are you available?"

Eve threw back her head and laughed, exposing her lovely throat. Mitch sat up in his chair and squelched the urge to climb over there and choke the guy.

"Define *available*," she teased. "Wouldn't you say it takes a lot of man to play second fiddle to all of you?"

A woman in a pink dress wrestled the microphone out of the young man's hand and spoke into it breathlessly. "I saw a picture of him—that man you were dating. If you've turned him loose, could you send him my way, please?"

The audience cracked up, and so did Eve. When she could speak, she said, "He's fine, isn't he?" She glanced at him, her face alive with laughter. "Mitch, stand up and take a bow." He got up and waved at the woman in pink, and saw his own face appear on the monitor. "Folks, this is Mitchell Hayes, and he used to work for one of the networks bidding on the show."

"Mitchell! Mitchell!" The audience began to chant. "Mitchell!"

Eve beckoned with one hand. "Come on up," she mouthed.

He should have expected this. After all the DVD footage he'd watched, he should have known that anything might happen at one of these town-hall shows.

A PA ran out with a stool and a third wireless microphone, and he made himself comfortable next to Eve.

"How do you feel about the news, Mitchell?" With the spotlight in his eyes, he couldn't see much, but the monitor off to the left showed a guy in a suit. "Does it make you feel weird that the woman you're seeing is illegitimate?"

Wow. He took that one right in the solar plexus and drew in a breath.

"Legally, I don't think she is. But it's irrelevant to me." He turned and gave the rest of his answer to Eve. "The woman I see is talented, beautiful and has a family who adores and protects her. I'm not sure what she sees in me, but I'm crazy in love with her."

Under lashes heavy with stage makeup, Eve's eyes widened.

"Atlanta, you're lucky to have her," he went on. "And so am I."

Huge applause, and a few wolf whistles.

"Are you still with the network?" the next person wanted to know. He barely heard the question. He was too busy watching that beautiful face, those eyes that were shiny with tears and filling with everything she wanted to say and couldn't. Not out here in public, with cameras and people and half of the South listening in.

Okay, so it hadn't been fair to out them so completely, in front of all those thousands of viewers. And yet, it had seemed absolutely the right thing to do.

Something that would only happen on *Just Between Us*.

The volunteer repeated his question, and Mitch finally dragged his gaze from Eve's face. "No, I'm not," he said. "I'm happy to say that I'm the new director of business development for the Ashmere Trust." Beside him, Eve gasped, and he turned. He couldn't get enough of looking at her. "In fact, we're throwing a benefit next Saturday night at Mirabel, which you may or may not know is the plantation that Eve's family owned up until the sixties." He returned his gaze to the cameras. "I'd like to invite all of you to join us in support of a new program in Atlanta. It's called Music on the Street."

Eve made a choked noise, and covered her mouth as the tears spilled over. Happy tears, he knew that. Tears of celebration that sparkled on her cheeks like diamonds.

He grinned and took the hand of the woman who had made all his dreams come true, and together, they turned their faces toward the spotlights.

Epilogue

JENNA HAMILTON CLOSED her office door with a sense of satisfaction, shutting out the buzz of activity in the offices of Andersen Nadeau.

She'd just spent the last half hour with a hard-nosed fireplug called Nelson Berg, who had been handed off to her by Eve Best when he'd made a pest of himself at CATL-TV. He'd come here with ultimatums and too much testosterone, and had left with a contract and a greater respect for the negotiating power of a woman.

Jenna smiled. That man hadn't met a hardnose until he'd met her.

Just Between Us would be staying in Atlanta, broadcast by CWB. Score one for the little guys.

Now that the show's future was taken care of, she had to make another trip to the law library and continue digging for precedent on lottery cases. Despite her feeling of buoyancy about her success with the CWB negotiation, she had no illusions about the possibility of losing this case for Eve and her friends. Twice now, she'd picked up her phone to call the senior partner and admit that, while she was darned good at corporate law and contracts, she didn't have the experience for this.

To ask him to have her reassigned, and give the case to someone who actually knew what they were doing and could pull it off.

But she'd disconnected before she went through with it.

Both Nicole Reavis and Jane Kurtz had called her yesterday in a panic, saying they'd arrived home to find a letter from Lot'O'Bucks. In it, the state lottery board was reminding the women that they had only eight months from the time of the announcement of their win to collect their money. Already, nearly three months had been eaten away because of the lawsuit.

The clock ticked with relentless disregard for deadlines, and Jenna was no closer to reaching a solution than she had been during those first dreadful weeks when Liza had returned to announce she wanted her fair share.

There was one tiny bright spot in this gloom, however. The Lot'O'Bucks ultimatum gave her a perfect reason to call Kevin Wade.

She took the elevator down to the lobby, where there was an espresso bar, and fortified herself with a double-shot, no-whip latte. It wouldn't last long, but at least it cleared her brain enough to communicate like a mature woman, instead of the breathless idiot she seemed to become when she talked with him. At least on the phone, she wouldn't be distracted by those warm brown eyes and the hot focus she saw in them. Or that mouth that spoke Latin terms and precedents when it should be making pillow talk and kissing her.

Ow. Back in her office, Jenna stubbed her patent-leather toe on the leg of her rolling desk chair.

So much for not being distracted.

She took another hit of the latte, sat and dialed his number.

"Jenna," he said with satisfaction as soon as he heard her voice. "I was just thinking about you."

Part of her melted. The rational part said, "Oh? Did your client get a letter from Lot'O'Bucks, too?"

He chuckled. "As a matter of fact, she did. This steps up the pressure a bit, doesn't it?"

"It does. But I'd prefer not to drag it out, in any case. Is your client more inclined now to come to a settlement agreement?"

"Are yours?"

"I asked you first."

"Then I would have to say no. Remember that in *Karpik v. Post,* the judge awarded the claimant a percentage of the winnings."

"That case isn't relevant to ours. Even though they went in on the tickets together, they didn't choose the numbers together. The complainant just bought a batch of tickets with the defendant's money."

Kevin chuckled. "Can't put a single thing past you, can I?"

"I've memorized every case I've been able to find having anything to do with a lottery, ever," she admitted. "Along with work on my other corporate clients, I'm getting a bit fried."

"Me, too. Why don't you take a break and meet me?"

Well, at least it was nice to know they were on the same wavelength. That she wasn't just having a sweet fantasy, all by herself.

"Kevin, you know we can't while we're on opposing sides of this case."

"You said that the other week and met me anyway. And didn't we have a good time—until you got cold feet and ran off on me?"

Her whole body sighed at the thought. "Yes. But it can't happen again. Look, I admit I'm very attracted to you. But I'm not willing to risk my success on this case by setting up a possible ethics problem. You understand."

After a moment, he said, "I do. But that doesn't make it any easier. I've been thinking about you ever since."

"Likewise."

"So what are we going to do about it? Are you going to send me on my merry way?"

"I'd rather not," she said carefully. He probably had flocks of salivating women on speed dial. It wouldn't take more than five minutes for a man like that to find someone to spend his time with. "But I don't see any way past it."

"I do."

Gee, a virtual affair. Lovely.

She dropped her voice, even though the walls were thick in this old building. "I'm not having some kind of online e-mail sex thing. Absolutely not."

His laugh startled her. "Hey, what do you take me for, a teenage geek? No, I simply meant that I'm willing to wait until after this case is over to see you on anything more than a professional basis."

He was? His voice had become as soft as melted sugar. Man, was she ever in trouble.

"I feel as though I'd sat down to this wonderful feast," he murmured, "and after I took one bite, someone took the plate away."

Come on, there wasn't a thing a girl could say to something like *that*. "You do?" she managed to reply.

"I'm willing to wait, so that I can enjoy that wonderful feast to the fullest when it's the right time for me to do it," he said. "What about you?"

With you to look forward to, five months is nothing.

No, no, she couldn't say that. A girl had to have some pride.

"After all, what's five months when there's someone like you at the end of it?" he asked softly.

Oh, man. If he was reading her mind, she was done for. "I'll make it worth your while when we get there," she promised.

"I'll hold you to that." He chuckled, and added, "Meantime, see you in negotiations."

And suddenly, the prospect of yet more negotiations took on a golden glow. True, she had a ton of work to do. More wakeful nights. More meetings with Eve and the other winners at the station. But at the end of it all lay the prospect of victory—for her, and for the people she represented.

She refused to consider any other outcome.

"You will," she promised, a smile warming her voice. "And may the best lawyer win."

* * * * *

*Don't miss
Kate Hoffmann's
FOR LUST OR MONEY—
the next installment in*
MILLION DOLLAR SECRETS
coming in October from Harlequin Blaze!

For a sneak preview of Marie Ferrarella's
DOCTOR IN THE HOUSE,
coming to NEXT in September,
please turn the page.

He didn't look like an unholy terror.

But maybe that reputation was exaggerated, Bailey DelMonico thought as she turned in her chair to look toward the doorway.

The man didn't seem scary at all.

Dr. Munro, or Ivan the Terrible, was tall, with an athletic build and wide shoulders. The cheekbones beneath what she estimated to be day-old stubble were prominent. His hair was light brown and just this side of unruly. Munro's hair looked as if he used his fingers for a comb and didn't care who knew it.

The eyes were brown, almost black as they were aimed at her. There was no other word for it. Aimed. As if he was debating whether or not to fire at point-blank range.

Somewhere in the back of her mind, a line from a B movie, "Be afraid—be very afraid…" whispered along the perimeter of her brain. Warning her. Almost against her will, it caused her to brace her shoulders. Bailey had to remind herself to breathe in and out like a normal person.

The chief of staff, Dr. Bennett, had tried his level best

to put her at ease and had almost succeeded. But an air of tension had entered with Munro. She wondered if Dr. Bennett was bracing himself as well, bracing for some kind of disaster or explosion.

"Ah, here he is now," Harold Bennett announced needlessly. The smile on his lips was slightly forced, and the look in his gray, kindly eyes held a warning as he looked at his chief neurosurgeon. "We were just talking about you, Dr. Munro."

"Can't imagine why," Ivan replied dryly.

Harold cleared his throat, as if that would cover the less than friendly tone of voice Ivan had just displayed. "Dr. Munro, this is the young woman I was telling you about yesterday."

Now his eyes dissected her. Bailey felt as if she was undergoing a scalpel-less autopsy right then and there. "Ah yes, the Stanford Special."

He made her sound like something that was listed at the top of a third-rate diner menu. There was enough contempt in his voice to offend an entire delegation from the UN.

Summoning the bravado that her parents always claimed had been infused in her since the moment she first drew breath, Bailey put out her hand. "Hello. I'm Dr. Bailey DelMonico."

Ivan made no effort to take the hand offered to him. Instead, he slid his long, lanky form bonelessly into the chair beside her. He proceeded to move the chair ever so slightly so that there was even more space between them. Ivan faced the chief of staff, but the words he spoke were addressed to her.

"You're a doctor, DelMonico, when I say you're a doctor," he informed her coldly, sparing her only one frosty glance to punctuate the end of his statement.

Harold stifled a sigh. "Dr. Munro is going to take over your education. Dr. Munro—" he fixed Ivan with a steely gaze that had been known to send lesser doctors running for their antacids, but, as always, seemed to have no effect on the chief neurosurgeon "—I want you to award her every consideration. From now on, Dr. DelMonico is to be your shadow, your sponge and your assistant." He emphasized the last word as his eyes locked with Ivan's. "Do I make myself clear?"

For his part, Ivan seemed completely unfazed. He merely nodded, his eyes and expression unreadable. "Perfectly."

His hand was on the doorknob. Bailey sprang to her feet. Her chair made a scraping noise as she moved it back and then quickly joined the neurosurgeon before he could leave the office.

Closing the door behind him, Ivan leaned over and whispered into her ear, "Just so you know, I'm going to be your worst nightmare."

Bailey DelMonico has finally
gotten her life on track, and is
passionate about her recent career
change. Nothing will stand in the way
of her becoming a doctor...that is,
until she's paired with the sharp-tongued
Dr. Ivan Munro.

Watch the sparks fly in

Doctor in
the House

by *USA TODAY* Bestselling Author

Marie Ferrarella

Available September 2007

Intrigued? Read more at
TheNextNovel.com

HARLEQUIN®

N_xt™

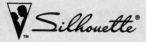

Romantic
SUSPENSE

Sparked by Danger,
Fueled by Passion.

When evidence is found that Mallory Dawes
intends to sell the personal financial information
of government employees to "the Russian,"
OMEGA engages undercover agent Cutter Smith.
Tailing her all the way to France, Cutter is
fighting a growing attraction to Mallory while at
the same time having to determine her connection
to "the Russian." Is Mallory really the mouse in
this game of cat and mouse?

Look for

Stranded with a Spy

by *USA TODAY* bestselling author

Merline Lovelace

October 2007.

Also available October wherever you buy books:

BULLETPROOF MARRIAGE *(Mission: Impassioned)*
by Karen Whiddon

A HERO'S REDEMPTION *(Haven)* by Suzanne McMinn

TOUCHED BY FIRE by Elizabeth Sinclair

REQUEST YOUR FREE BOOKS!

2 FREE NOVELS PLUS 2 FREE GIFTS!

HARLEQUIN®

Blaze

Red-hot reads!

YES! Please send me 2 FREE Harlequin® Blaze® novels and my 2 FREE gifts. After receiving them, if I don't wish to receive any more books, I can return the shipping statement marked "cancel." If I don't cancel, I will receive 6 brand-new novels every month and be billed just $3.99 per book in the U.S., or $4.47 per book in Canada, plus 25¢ shipping and handling per book and applicable taxes, if any*. That's a savings of at least 15% off the cover price! I understand that accepting the 2 free books and gifts places me under no obligation to buy anything. I can always return a shipment and cancel at any time. Even if I never buy another book from Harlequin, the two free books and gifts are mine to keep forever.

151 HDN EF3W   351 HDN EF3X

Name	(PLEASE PRINT)	
Address		Apt.
City	State/Prov.	Zip/Postal Code

Signature (if under 18, a parent or guardian must sign)

Mail to the **Harlequin Reader Service®:**
IN U.S.A.: P.O. Box 1867, Buffalo, NY 14240-1867
IN CANADA: P.O. Box 609, Fort Erie, Ontario L2A 5X3

Not valid to current Harlequin Blaze subscribers.

Want to try two free books from another line?
Call 1-800-873-8635 or visit www.morefreebooks.com.

* Terms and prices subject to change without notice. NY residents add applicable sales tax. Canadian residents will be charged applicable provincial taxes and GST. This offer is limited to one order per household. All orders subject to approval. Credit or debit balances in a customer's account(s) may be offset by any other outstanding balance owed by or to the customer. Please allow 4 to 6 weeks for delivery.

Your Privacy: Harlequin is committed to protecting your privacy. Our Privacy Policy is available online at www.eHarlequin.com or upon request from the Reader Service. From time to time we make our lists of customers available to reputable firms who may have a product or service of interest to you. If you would prefer we not share your name and address, please check here. ☐

HB07

HARLEQUIN®
Blaze™

COMING NEXT MONTH

www.eHarlequin.com

HBCNM0907